Bumpy Roads

A MARY O'REILLY PARANORMAL MYSTERY

By Terri Reid

"If you live to be a hundred, I want to live to be a hundred minus one day so I never have to live without you."

"If ever there is tomorrow when we're not together... there is something you must always remember. You are braver than you believe, stronger than you seem, and smarter than you think. But the most important thing is, even if we're apart... I'll always be with you."

"How lucky I am to have something that makes saying goodbye so hard."

"I think we dream so we don't have to be apart for so long. If we're in each other's dreams, we can be together all the time."

~*The Adventures of Christopher Robin*, A.A. Milne

We all grieve when we lose someone we love, but often it is hard for children who have not only lost their loved one, but also their security. Grief and depression often go hand in hand in children. If you love a child who has lost someone, please be sure to help them through their journey of grief. Allow them to express their feelings and help them to feel safe.

BUMPY ROADS – A MARY O'REILLY
PARANORMAL MYSTERY

by Terri Reid

Copyright © 2013 by Terri Reid

The author would like to thank all those who have contributed to the creation of this book: Richard Reid, Sarah Reid, Richard Onines, Virginia Onines, Elise Brubaker and Cyndy Ranzau.

And especially to the wonderful readers who walk with me through Mary and Bradley's adventures and encourage me along the way. Thank you all!

Prologue

Eight years ago

The air was heavy with humidity and dark storm clouds were moving east toward Freeport. Softball practice had run late and four teenage girls, all best friends, stood next to the bleachers picking up their gear and chatting about the upcoming prom. Courtney Rasmussen lifted her long brown hair up, so the wind could reach the back of her neck. "I sure hope the storm cools things down," she said.

Beth Anne Lloyd, whose short curls blew around her face, laughed. "It will probably just get more humid," she said, rolling her eyes. "You've got to love spring in Illinois."

Courtney stuffed her windbreaker into her backpack before slinging it over her shoulder. "Well, I'm okay with spring because that means summer isn't too far away. Hey, I'm going shopping on Saturday for my prom dress," she said. "So, if anyone wants to come along, we've got room in the van."

Ellie Martinson grinned. "Sure, I'll go," she said. "And I'll see if my mom will let me bring her credit card."

She wagged her eyebrows. "Things could get very interesting," she said.

The others laughed and, by some unspoken agreement, all started to walk toward the parking lot. "Hey, Courtney," Beth Anne asked, as she stopped

1

by her car. "Do you want a ride home? It looks like the storm could start any minute."

Courtney shook her head. "No, that's okay," she said. "I'm just on the other side of the park. I'll make it home before the rain."

Glancing up to the sky, she realized that she had better hurry or she would be caught in the early spring downpour. "I'll see you guys tomorrow," she called, jogging backward across the parking lot toward the path that led to the back of the park. "Don't get wet."

She turned and started to run toward the back entrance of the park. A cold wind blew, scattering the leaves that lay in the gutters alongside the path. Yellow Creek bordered this side of the park, separating it from the wooded residential area tucked into an exclusive area of Freeport. The wide pathways merged into streets bordered by large lawns with small thickets of trees. Most of the homes were pushed back, far away from the road, with large front yards.

Hurrying to the old bridge that crossed Yellow Creek, Courtney stepped to the side as a car came up behind her. The bridge was only wide enough for one car and even foot traffic had to climb up on the narrow ledge for safety. The car slowed and the driver's side window rolled down. A familiar face greeted Courtney.

"Hey, Courtney, how about a ride?" he asked.

She shook her head. "No thanks, I'm good," she said. "It's only a few more blocks."

The driver looked up to the sky. "You won't make it before the storm hits," he argued. "Come on, I'll feel guilty all night if I leave you here."

She smiled. "Okay, if you put it that way," she agreed, jogging over to the passenger side of the car and letting herself in.

The door lock clicked as she buckled her seatbelt and she looked up in surprise. "It does that automatically," the driver said with an apologetic shrug.

He shifted the car, but instead of moving smoothly forward, it sputtered and died. Looking over to his passenger, he grinned. "How embarrassing," he said. "Just give me a minute."

He pulled the key out of the ignition and put it on the dashboard. "It just has to cool down," he said. "Then I can start it again."

Outside, the sky darkened and the beat of fat drops of rain echoed against the roof of the car. The air inside the car seemed stuffy and hot. "I'm so glad you decided to come with me, Courtney," the driver said. "I would have hated for you to be caught in this deluge."

He reached over and ran his hand up her arm. "You would have been soaked to the skin," he whispered softly, his eyes slowly glancing over her body. "Your clothes would have been like a second skin."

Courtney scooted against the door and grasped the handle. "You know, I think I'll just walk anyway," she said, pulling against the handle.

But the door didn't open. She tried it again, but it was still locked tight.

"Child locks," the driver said, a smile on his face. "You can't get out until I let you out."

She pressed the window button, but it also stayed in place. "Listen, I don't want to be in this car," she said firmly. "Now please let me out or I'm going to scream."

He chuckled softly, leaned forward and placed his hand against her cheek, rubbing it intimately. "If you scream, no one will hear you," he said, as he slipped his hand down to her neck. "But you can do it if you like. I always love to hear a girl's scream."

Chapter One

Bradley pulled the car up into Mary's driveway and shifted into park. He turned and looked at Mary, his new wife, sitting next to him and smiled. "You know, once I turn the car off and we step outside, the honeymoon is over," he said.

She shook her head and smiled up at him, her love shining through her eyes. "Bradley, our honeymoon is never going to end."

He leaned forward and threaded his fingers through her hair, cradling her head. "How did I ever get so lucky?" he murmured, as he bent down for a gentle kiss.

She wrapped her arms around his neck and grinned. "You keep this up and you're really going to get lucky," she teased.

Breaking off the kiss, he quickly unhooked his seatbelt, got out of the car and opened her door. "Come on," he said, extending his hand toward her.

"Where?"

"Into the house," he replied, bending over and pressing a quick kiss on her lips. "So you can show me how lucky a guy can get."

"But the luggage," she said.

He reached over and unbuckled her seatbelt. "Yeah, it can wait," he said, taking her hand and helping her out of the car.

She smiled up at him. "How long until Clarissa gets home?" she asked, slipping out of the car and walking toward the house. "I'm still on Scotland time."

Glancing at his watch, he answered, "We have three hours, plenty of time."

Sending him a saucy look over her shoulder, she paused for a moment in the front yard. "Maybe, if we hurry."

The surprised look in his face changed instantly to one of delight as he quickly locked the car doors and hurried after her. With a happy squeal, she ran across the lawn and up the porch stairs. She was nearly to the door, when he caught her, spun her around and kissed her.

"Mmmm," she purred. "Welcome home."

He bent down and scooped her into his arms.

"I can walk," she reminded him.

He kissed her again. "Yes, but I have to carry you over the threshold, it's my husbandly duty," he said, punching in the security code and unlocking the door.

Mary winked at him and unbuttoned the top button of his shirt. "Well hurry and open the door, so you can put me down and concentrate on more interesting husbandly duties."

"I'm not putting you down…" he exclaimed with a smoldering look, as he pushed the door open, "until I drop you on the mattress."

"SURPRISE!"

Bradley and Mary looked up to find their home filled with their friends.

"Oh, my," Mary said, biting her lower lip in embarrassment.

"Hey, don't worry," Mike said, appearing next to them. "We didn't hear Bradley say anything about a mattress."

She buried her head in his shoulder and felt the rise and fall of Bradley's chest as he began to laugh. He bent down and nuzzled her ear. "Welcome home, darling."

She looked up at him, saw the tender humor in his eyes and laughed too. "Yes, welcome home."

An hour later, as they sat together around the kitchen table, Ian tapped his spoon on the side of his teacup to quiet the group.

"What? Do you want us to kiss?" Bradley asked, winking at Mary and sighing. "If I must..."

"I dinna think you need any of my encouragement in that manner," Ian said. "Aye, according to the staff in Scotland, they nary saw hide nor hair of you for the entire week."

"Ian," Gillian reprimanded, a twinkle in her eye, "that wasn't very nice."

"I thought the sign of a good staff was discretion," Bradley teased.

"Well, they know who's paying their salaries, now don't they?" Ian replied with a smile. "But I understand I'm in debt to you."

"Whatever for?" Mary asked.

7

"Well, I understand that Headless Hannah is no longer walking the halls of the manor house," he replied.

"And that's a wonderful thing," Gillian added.

"Oh, Hannah," Mary said. "She was delightful. And she had such a great sense of humor."

Bradley shrugged. "I don't know about that," he said. "She kept winking at me. And let me tell you, it's disconcerting as hell having a head on a platter winking at you."

"It's just that she caught you in…" She paused and sent an apologetic glance to Bradley.

Bradley groaned softly.

"In his what?" Stanley asked.

"Nothing," Bradley said. "Never mind."

"In his pajamas?" Rosie asked. "In his bed? In his chair?"

"I think you had just better tell them," Mary said apologetically.

Sighing, Bradley leaned back in his chair. "In my altogether," he replied.

"Your altogether what?" Rosie asked.

"He was naked," Stanley said. "He was trotting around Ian's castle naked."

"He wasn't trotting around naked," Mary protested. "He was just dancing naked in our room."

Ian grinned. "Dancing naked?" he snorted. "Why Bradley, there's more to you than meets the eye."

"Obviously not Mary's eye," Mike quipped.

8

"Anyway," Mary interrupted. "If not for your excellent research, we wouldn't have been able to discern the cause of her death. So, you don't owe us anything."

"How did she die?" Rosie asked.

"Part of the south wall of the estate collapsed in the early 1400s," Mary said.

"Aye, I remember the excavation we did on the grounds," Ian said. "We found a treasure trove of artifacts."

"Did you find a lot of old weapons?" Bradley asked.

"As a matter of fact, we did," Ian said.

"Poor Hannah happened to be standing near a display of treasured armaments when the wall came down," Mary explained. "Her decapitation was just an accident. No one murdered her. But because her death was so sudden, she had become stuck here on earth."

Rosie rubbed her neck. "That sounds awful," she said.

"Didn't look very pleasant either," Bradley added, reaching over and taking Mary's hand. "But it was nice to watch her find the light and move on."

Mary turned to him and nodded. "It was, wasn't it?"

They stared into each other's eyes for several moments until Ian finally cleared his throat and stood up. "Why, now, look at the time," he said loudly. "Stanley, Rosie, weren't you going to show Gillian and meself that thing down at your store?"

9

Rosie stood up and grinned at Ian. "Oh, thank you for reminding me," she said. "Of course, we were."

"What thing?" Stanley asked. "What are you talking about?"

Rosie grabbed Stanley's shoulder and pulled him out of his chair. "I'll remind you on the way over to the store," she said pointedly. "While Bradley and Mary have a little time to get settled."

"Settled?" Stanley argued. "Mary's lived here for more than two years. What the hell does she need time to get settled fer?"

"She wasn't a newlywed," Rosie said slowly.

Eyes slowly widening, Stanley blushed. "Oh, well, then, why didn't you say so?" he said. "Iffen these two want to make hay while the sun shines they should've scooted us out of this house a long time ago."

"Stanley, scoot," Bradley laughed, while Mary hid her face against his shoulder. "And don't let the door hit you on your way out."

When the door finally closed, Mike turned to the newlyweds and smiled. "Remember, this is Tuesday, so you've got about an hour before Clarissa gets home," he said. "I'll see what I can do to delay the bus a little."

Once he faded out in front of them, Bradley turned to Mary. "Hopefully that's the last of our surprises for the day," he said with a sigh.

Mary stood up and walked toward the staircase. Halfway there, she turned and smiled at

10

him over her shoulder. "Oh, I don't know," she said with a seductive tone. "There might be another one or two waiting for you upstairs."

Chapter Two

Clarissa looked out the window of the bus, her stomach clenched with anticipation as they pulled away from the school. Her best friend Maggie, seated next to her, was unaware of her friend's tension. "It's so exciting," she gushed. "Mary and Bradley are probably already home."

Clarissa's stomach tensed again. "Yes, I know."

"This is so great," Maggie continued. "Now we both have a family and we live almost next door to each other."

Clarissa turned in her seat. "Maggie, my mom and dad used to tell me that they loved me more because they chose me," she said. "I wasn't just born to them; they found me so I would always be special."

Nodding, Maggie smiled. "That's kind of what my parents tell me," she said.

"But Mary and Bradley didn't choose me," Maggie said. "I heard people talking at the wedding about how surprised Bradley was to learn I was alive."

"But it was a good surprise, right?" Maggie asked.

Shrugging, Clarissa looked back out the window. "I don't know," she said quietly. "I don't know if it was a good surprise or…"

"Or what?"

"The lady at the wedding said I was an obligation," Clarissa replied. "And it wasn't fair that Mary had to raise someone else's child."

"What's an obligation?" Maggie asked.

"I looked it up in the dictionary," Clarissa said. "It's like a debt, something you have to take care of, even if you don't want to."

Thinking back to her babysitter in Chicago, Clarissa could almost hear Mrs. Gunderson's voice screaming, *It's your fault your mother is sick. If you weren't around, she could rest and get better. You're just sucking the life right out of her.*

"But…but…you're Bradley's daughter and he loves you," Maggie said, interrupting Clarissa's thoughts.

"My mom said she loved me too," Clarissa said. "But I sucked the life right out of her."

"What?" Maggie asked. "Your mom was sick – that's why she died."

"I miss my mom," Clarissa said, her lower lip trembling. "I miss my mom and my dad. I wish they were still here."

"But you never talk about them," Maggie said, surprised at her friend's words. "You never acted like you missed them."

Wiping away a few stray tears, Clarissa took a deep breath. "That's because I'm not supposed to talk

13

about them. I'm supposed to pretend I was always Mary and Bradley's little girl and didn't have another mom and dad. I didn't want to make them mad and tell me to go because I was afraid the bad man would get me."

"Why are you s'posed to pretend?" Maggie asked.

"The lady on the bus from Chicago told me that people don't want a little girl who's always sad, so if I wanted to make my new family happy, I needed to pretend that everything was just fine. She told me to just forget about my mom."

"It would be hard to forget about your mom," Maggie said.

Clarissa shook her head. "You can let your inside cry, but your outside has to be happy."

"But didn't your Grandma O'Reilly tell you it was okay to cry?" Maggie asked.

"But she's a grandma, so that's different," Clarissa decided. "I'm not her obligation. I just have to be happy for Mary."

Maggie considered that for a moment. "I don't think so," she said, matter-of-factly. "I think she just wants you to be you. I really think she loves you."

"Maybe she does or maybe she doesn't have a choice," Clarissa said. "Maybe they'll just get tired of me and send me away."

"I don't believe that," Maggie said. "Mary loves you. Mary loves everybody. Besides, I heard my mom tell my dad that Mary can't have babies. So, she's pretty lucky she has you."

Clarissa looked at Maggie. "Really? She can't?" she asked, a hesitant smile on her face.

"That's what my mom said. She said it was 'cause of the time she got shot when she was worked for the police."

"Did it hurt?" Clarissa asked.

Nodding her head urgently, Maggie replied. "She even died. But she got sent back to earth."

"Why?"

"So she could help people."

"That's nice," Clarissa said and pausing for a moment, she crossed her fingers and prayed the lie she was going to say wouldn't really count. "I'm sorry she can't have babies."

Maybe they'll want me, she thought. *Maybe because they can't have babies they'll need me.*

The knot in her stomach loosened and she was finally excited about going home to see her new mom and dad. Her new family. Just the three of them, for now and always.

15

Chapter Three

Bradley and Mary were waiting in the doorway when the bus pulled up in front of their house. As Clarissa alighted and saw them waiting for her, she paused for a moment and then ran to them, her arms outstretched. "You're home," she cried. "You're finally home."

Bradley picked her up and he and Mary hugged her. "I think you've grown three inches since we saw you," he said.

Giggling, Clarissa shook her head. "No, I haven't," she replied, "but I did lose a tooth."

"A tooth?" Mary exclaimed. "Let me see."

Clarissa obligingly opened her mouth as wide as she could and pointed to the empty spot where her tooth used to be. "Ight air," she said, keeping her mouth open.

"Right there?" Bradley questioned.

She nodded, her eyes shining brightly.

"Well, that's just amazing," Mary said. "Did the tooth fairy come yet?"

"No, I was waiting for you to get home," she explained, shaking her head for emphasis. "Mrs. Brennan said that would be okay."

"It's more than okay," Mary said, rubbing the little girl's head gently. "It's perfect. I've always wanted to meet the tooth fairy."

Bradley looked up suddenly and stared at Mary, concern written on his face. She grinned and shook her head, mouthing the words, "I'm kidding," over Clarissa's head. He was visibly relieved.

"Well, I've always wanted to meet her too," he said, a note of teasing now in his voice. "So, what do we do first? Set a trap?"

Mary and Clarissa glanced at each other and rolled their eyes. "No, you don't trap the tooth fairy," Clarissa explained.

"Unless you want cavities in all of your teeth," Mary added.

"Oh, so what do you do?" he asked, carrying Clarissa into the house and depositing her on a chair at the kitchen table.

He pulled up a chair next to her and gave her all of his attention.

Mary stood back, next to the counter and watched as her husband listened carefully to Clarissa as she explained, in great detail, the intricacies of getting a tooth fairy to pick up your tooth and leave a gift. He shook his head often and murmured appropriate responses throughout the conversation, and Mary fell a little bit more in love with him.

Finally, when the conversation was over, they both looked over to her expectantly. "I'm sorry," she said. "Did I miss something?"

"We need a container," Clarissa explained. "For my tooth."

"Ah," Mary replied, nodding slowly. "Something very special and very small, right?"

They both agreed.

Reaching up, she opened a cabinet and stood on her tiptoes and pulled out a cardboard box. She placed the box on the counter and took the top off. "This is my treasure box," she said. "It has all kinds of special things I saved when I was a little girl. I think I have exactly what we need in here."

Rustling through the box, she finally located a tiny bone china chest with a lid that opened and closed. She picked it up and held it out to Clarissa. "Well, what do you think?" she asked. "Will this do?"

Jumping from her chair, the child hurried over to Mary and gently took hold of the chest. With wonder she opened and closed the lid several times, latching and unlatching the tiny hook that held it in place. "This is perfect," she said. "Can I really use it?"

"You can use it and you can keep it," Mary said, "as long as you take good care of it."

Lunging forward, she wrapped her arms around Mary and hugged her. "I'll take good care of it," she said. "I promise."

Bending over, Mary placed a kiss on Clarissa's head. "I'm sure you will."

Bradley came over and knelt next to Clarissa, examining the chest in her hand. "That chest looks sturdy enough to handle a hundred teeth. One at a time, of course," he said.

"That's silly," Clarissa said. "My teacher said kids only lose twenty teeth, not a hundred."

"Well, how about your brothers or sisters," Bradley teased. "If you don't mind sharing with them."

Clarissa's face sobered and she studied both of her parents. "What brothers and sisters?" she asked.

Laughing, Bradley gave her a quick hug. "I know you're going to love being a big sister," he said.

"Well, let's not get the cart before the horse," Mary inserted. "We don't even know if we can have babies."

"You're going to have a baby?" Clarissa asked, her voice rising slightly.

"No, dear," Mary soothed. "No I'm not going to have a baby."

"Not yet, anyway," Bradley said with a smile. "But won't it be great when she does?"

Clarissa swallowed audibly and slowly nodded her head. "I guess so," she said. "But what about…"

Bradley bent over and kissed her forehead. "Why don't you go on upstairs and get changed," he interrupted. "Then we can show you what we brought you back from Scotland."

"Oh, okay," she replied, turning away from them and slowly walking up the stairs.

"Clarissa," Mary called. "You forgot the chest."

She obediently turned around and took the chest from Mary's hand. "Thanks," she replied half-heartedly.

"Put your tooth in it and place it on your nightstand, and I'm sure the tooth fairy will pick it up tonight," Mary promised.

Clarissa sighed deeply. "Okay," she said. "I will."

She walked away again, her head bowed and her steps heavy. They watched her walk up the stairs in silence. "What do you think is wrong?" Bradley asked.

Mary shook her head. "I have a feeling we are going to have some interesting adjustments as we create our new family."

Clarissa climbed the stairs, walked to her room, closed the door and sat on the edge of her bed. She placed the little chest down on her nightstand, dropped her backpack on the floor and rolled onto her bed, curling up into a fetal position as tears fell from her eyes.

You're nothing but trouble. No one wants you. Mrs. Gunderson's voice echoed in her mind. *You're the reason your parents are dead – do you think anyone wants you to be part of their family?*

"No!" she cried out loud. "They want me. I'll make them want me."

Chapter Four

The alarm went off and Mary, her eyes still closed, automatically reached across the bed to turn it off. But instead of finding her nightstand and the clock, her hand encountered flesh – warm, breathing flesh. Eyes popping open immediately, she turned her head and was initially surprised by the man lying in bed next to her. But, as her mind finally caught up with the rest of her, she remembered that the large expanse of male softly snoring in her bed was her new husband. Reaching over him, she quickly clicked off the buzzing alarm.

She levered herself up on a bent arm to watch him sleep. Leaning forward, she brushed his hair from his forehead and softly feathered her fingers through his hair. He smiled in his sleep and she grinned back. She bent forward to place a kiss on his forehead when strong arms wrapped around her and pulled her across the bed into his embrace. She nestled her head against his neck. "Morning," she whispered, placing her lips against his collarbone.

"Morning," he said, his morning voice deep and hoarse.

He leaned back, looked down at her with a smile on his lips and bent forward to kiss her. She ducked and burrowed against his shoulder. "No, you can't kiss me yet," she exclaimed. "I have morning breath. Gross!"

She could feel the chuckle reverberate throughout his body. "Do we have to have gum or mints next to the bed?" he asked, nibbling on her neck.

She stretched, allowing him more access. "That would be nice," she agreed. "And maybe a little container of mouthwash."

He lifted his head. "What?"

"You know, mouthwash," she said. "And maybe some cups to spit in."

"Mary, you are ruining the mood," he replied, running his hand down the side of her body. "We need to be spontaneous."

She arched against him. "I'm spontaneous," she argued, her breathing becoming slightly erratic. "I'm just spontaneous with good dental hygiene."

He kissed her neck and her collarbone, spending time on the sensitive spot where her pulse beat wildly beneath her skin. "Mary," he breathed, as he began to move lower.

"Yes," she stammered, her eyes closed in pure delight.

Just then his cell phone rang. He swore softly and rolled over, slipped out from under the covers and walked across the room to the dresser. "Alden," he said as he answered the phone. "Yeah, Tom, what's up?"

Mary scooted up in bed and smiled, enjoying the fine picture her husband presented from the back.

22

All those months watching him stretch before they jogged. Yes, she sighed silently, he was even sexy under baggy cut-off sweats, but without them…damn!

He turned, caught her watching him and lifted an eyebrow in her direction. She grinned and sent him a double thumbs up. Choking back laughter, he turned away to pay attention to the call. "Sure, Tom, I can meet," he agreed. "Yeah, I can be there by seven-thirty this morning. No. No problem. Thanks."

He hung up the phone and turned around to face her. "I've got to go in early," he said, regret heavy in his voice.

"Back to the real world," she replied with a sigh. "I should get up too. I want to be fully awake when Clarissa comes down this morning so she can show us what the tooth fairy left her."

He climbed back into bed next to her and massaged her back. "Do you think we did it right?" he asked.

Stretching and enjoying his warm hands on her back, she leaned forward and sighed. "We did just fine," she said. "I only got a quarter; a dollar is more than enough."

"But this is her first tooth with us," he argued.

"Good thing I gave her that tiny chest or you would have wanted to put a bike under her pillow," she teased.

He pulled her backward into his arms and kissed her on the mouth. "Come on," he said. "We can shower together."

She shook her head innocently. "Oh, that's not necessary, we have plenty of time for each of us to have our own showers," she insisted.

Grabbing her hand and pulling her off the bed, he shook his head. "Not the way I was planning it."

Sometime later, dressed in a big white towel, Mary leaned against the bathroom doorframe. She looked at her towel-clad husband through the mirror, his face white with shaving cream, and smiled. "That was the best shower I've ever taken," she admitted.

He grinned back at her. "Me too," he replied and then he shook his head. "Mary, I'm really not ready to get back to the real world. Let's run away to Hawaii."

She came up behind him, wrapped her arms around his waist and laid her head against his back. "So, what part of today are you not looking forward to?" she asked, placing a kiss on his back.

"Oh, let's see, there's the meetings and the paperwork," he said. "And then there's the paperwork and the meetings."

"It's tough having a glamorous job like Chief of Police," she said. "But someone has to do it."

He turned in her arms and put his hand under her chin lifting her head slightly. "I really wish we didn't have to go back into the real world," he said, placing a kiss on her lips. "Should we run away to a tropical paradise?"

"Bugs," Mary said. "Big ones."

"That's true," he agreed. "Okay, I'll guess we'll stay here."

Reaching up and kissing him back, she grinned. "Good choice."

Chapter Five

"Good morning, Clarissa," Mary said, opening her daughter's bedroom door and peeking inside. "Your dad has to leave early this morning, but he didn't want to leave without saying goodbye to you. Are you ready to get up?"

Stretching and wiping the sleep out of her eyes, Clarissa nodded, slipped out of her bed, and started padding down the hall toward the stairs. "Don't you want to see what the tooth fairy left you?" Mary reminded her.

Eyes widening instantly, Clarissa hurried back to her room and stuck her hand underneath her pillow. She pulled out the little chest, excited to open it. In her hurry, the delicate piece slipped from her hands and fell onto the wooden floor. They both heard the crack at the same time. Clarissa froze and Mary hurried forward, picking up the pieces of chest from the floor.

"Don't move," she said, more sharply than she meant, because Clarissa was barefoot and she didn't want her to cut her feet. "I'll be right back."

As Mary hurried into the bathroom for a damp washcloth, Bradley came into the room. "What happened?" he asked.

A tear stole down Clarissa's cheek. "I accidently broke Mom's chest," she said.

26

"Oh, Clarissa," Bradley said, distress in his voice. "How did it happen?"

Coming back into the room, Mary shook her head. "It was just an accident," she said. "It slipped, that's all."

Bradley saw the sheen in Mary's eyes as she wiped the wood floor and knew this was upsetting her more than she was letting on. "Mary, we're a family now," he said. "We need to be honest with each other."

Shrugging, she sat up and shook her head, wiping away a stray tear. "My grandmother gave it to me before she died," she admitted. "So, I'm a little sad. But this is not Clarissa's fault. It truly was just an accident."

Clarissa's heart dropped "I'm so sorry, Mom," Clarissa sobbed. "Please don't hate me."

"Oh, darling, I don't hate you," she said, hugging her daughter. "Don't worry about it."

"I guess we'll have to get something with reinforced steel or rubber for the rest of the baby teeth in the Alden household," Bradley teased. "I have a feeling that butterfingers might be a family trait that I'll pass on to all of our children."

Mary laughed and smiled up at Bradley. "Well, in that case, I'm going to hide all of my breakable things."

Mary was laughing, but Clarissa remembered her own mother would laugh when her father was home. Then when he left, the pain would show on her face and she would lie down for a long time. Mary must hate her but didn't want her dad to know.

She shivered as she remembered back in Chicago when she dropped a candy dish at Mrs. Gunderson's house. Mrs. Gunderson had slapped her hard across her face and told her she was a stupid child. Mary probably thought she was a stupid child too. Was Mary going to slap her once her dad left?

Bradley knelt down next to Clarissa and gave her a hug. "I've got to go into the office early," he said. "But I'll see you tonight."

"Okay," Clarissa whispered. "Have a nice day."

Pulling Mary into his arms, Bradley kissed her and then tenderly looked down into her eyes. "I'm really going to miss you," he said.

Clarissa stomach tightened even more. He hadn't said he was going to miss her. Did he love Mary more than he loved her?

"I'll miss you too," Mary said, tenderly running her hand through his hair. "Be careful out there."

They kissed once again and then Bradley bent down and pressed a quick kiss on Clarissa's forehead. "Goodbye my lovely ladies," he said with a wink, before he left.

Hearing the door close, Mary sighed softly. "Well, this was an exciting way to begin our first day as a family, wasn't it?" she asked Clarissa with a smile. "Do you need me to help you get dressed?"

Shaking her head, Clarissa stepped away from Mary. "No, I'm fine," she said. "I'll just get ready."

"Okay, I'll get your lunch ready and then we can have breakfast together," Mary said, as she leaned down and gave Clarissa a quick hug. "I'll see you in a few minutes."

Clarissa watched Mary go down the stairs. When was Mary going to be angry? When was she going to yell at her?

She looked at the large shard of china she had placed on her nightstand that Mary hadn't thrown away. It was so delicate and so beautiful. Mary must hate her for sure.

Chapter Six

There was a quick knock on the front door while Mary was in the kitchen putting a bag lunch together for Clarissa. She wiped her hands on a towel and hurried to the door. Opening it, she smiled when she saw Ian and Gillian standing hand-in-hand at the door.

"Come in," she invited. "I was just getting things together for Clarissa."

"Oh, good, then we haven't missed her," Ian said. "We wanted to see her before we left town."

Mary sighed. "I'm going to really miss you," she said. "You were the best roommate I ever had."

Ian turned to Gillian. "She meant that only in the most platonic way," he assured her.

Gillian laughed. "Aye, I can see she only has eyes for Bradley," she said. "And it's good for you that she does."

He leaned over and kissed her. "And I only have eyes for you, my love," he said.

"What a charmer," Mary laughed as she headed back to the kitchen to pack the rest of Clarissa's lunch bag. "Clarissa should be down any minute and I know she's going to love seeing you."

"Hey, are you having a party and no one invited me?" Mike asked, appearing in the living room.

"Aye, it's a going-away party," Ian said. "Gillian and I are off to Chicago this morning."

Gillian looked around the room. "Who are you talking to?" she asked.

"Oh, it's Mike," Ian explained. "He's the angel I was telling you about."

"The good-looking one," Mike added.

"Aye, the poor disfigured fellow," Ian said. "I've never seen such an ugly bloke in my life."

Gillian watched a mirror float through the room and hover in front of Ian's face. Only Ian and Mary could see that Mike was holding it there, but Gillian understood the joke. "Oh, I think your angel disagrees with your evaluation of his looks," she laughed. "So, you are a handsome fellow, are you?"

The mirror moved up and down.

"How did you ever get a woman with brains?" Mike asked Ian.

Ian chuckled. "Mike wants to know how I got a woman with brains."

"Well now, I'm might be smart, but I'm shallow," she said. "I liked the way he filled out his shirt."

Ian put his arm around her waist, pulled her close and kissed her cheek. "I'm fine with shallow," he said. "As long as you stay with me."

She turned and kissed him back. "Forever."

"More mush," Mike groaned, a twinkle in his eye. "I feel like I walked into the end of a fairy tale. I'm going to go back upstairs and see if I can get Clarissa to move along."

"Thanks Mike," Mary said. "That would be helpful."

A few minutes later, Clarissa came down the stairs slowly, trying not to make eye contact with anyone until she saw that Ian was in the room. "Ian!" she exclaimed, running down the remaining stairs and throwing herself into his arms. "I'm so glad you're here."

He hugged her and spun her around. "Aye, darling, I'm glad I'm here too," he said. "I couldn't leave Freeport without saying goodbye to my best girl."

Gillian elbowed him. "Second best girl," he amended with a grin.

Clarissa froze. "You're leaving?" she asked, her voice echoing the surprised look on her face.

"Aye, we're heading down to Chicago for a wee bit," he said. "I'll be working at the University completing my research while Gillian finishes up her assignment. But I promise we'll come back to Freeport when we can."

Clarissa shook her head, panic rushing through her little body. "No, you can't leave," she cried. "I need you to be here. No one will protect me if you go."

Ian hugged her. "Darling, there are plenty of people here that will take care of you and protect you," he said. "Your amazing new mother, Mary, has protected me a number of times. I'm sure no monster is a match for her."

Clarissa looked over her shoulder to Mary in the kitchen and whispered, "She hates me."

"What did you say, darling?" Ian asked.

She took a deep shaky breath. "Nothing," she said. "I just don't want you to leave."

He hugged her. "I won't be too far away," he said. "Chicago's not very far at all, and I'll come and visit you whenever I can."

Tears brimming in her eyes, she nodded her head and stepped away from him. "Okay," she said softly. "Goodbye Ian."

"Hey sweetheart," Mary said, coming back into the room. "What would you like for breakfast?"

Clarissa stepped back, avoiding Mary's embrace and shrugged. "That's okay, you don't have to make me breakfast," she said. "I can just help myself."

Confused, Mary stood back as Clarissa helped herself to some toast and peanut butter and placed it in a sandwich bag. "You don't have to hurry that much, sweetheart; you have plenty of time to eat your breakfast," Mary said. "The bus won't be here for fifteen minutes."

Clarissa picked up the sack lunch Mary and placed it in her backpack. "I'm going over to the Brennans' to wait for the bus with them," she said.

"Oh," Mary said, disappointed. "I thought we could spend a little time together."

She's just saying that, Clarissa thought, *because Ian and Gillian are here. I know she hates me.*

33

Shaking her head, Clarissa walked over and slipped on her coat. "I promised Maggie," she said, hoping Mary couldn't see through her lie. "I have to hurry."

She picked up her backpack and hurried to the door. With her hand on the doorknob she turned back to the room. "Goodbye Ian, goodbye Gillian, I hope you have a good time in Chicago," she said and then she opened the door and hurried outside.

Mary turned to Ian and Gillian, her heart aching a little bit. "Did I do something wrong?" she asked.

"Not that I could see from here," Ian said. "Seems the lass has a bee in her bonnet."

"Maybe she just needs to get used to all of you being a family now," Gillian suggested. "She really has been through a lot."

Nodding, Mary took a deep breath and tried to smile. "You're right," she agreed. "She's been through more in the past few weeks than most of us can handle in a lifetime. We probably all just need a little adjusting."

"Aye, that's right," Ian agreed. "Things will be fine in no time. But if you need us, we're only a phone call away."

Reaching over and hugging Ian, she nodded. "I'm going to miss having you around," she said. "But it's nice to know you're making Chicago a safer city."

Ian grinned. "Aye, those library books don't stand a chance with me around."

"Take care of Sean for me," she said. "I don't know what's going on, but I could tell something was bothering him."

"Yes, I think we'll be able to help," he said, sending a sideways glance to Gillian. "Gillian has some ideas about his red-headed mystery woman."

"You do?" Mary asked her.

Gillian smiled. "Oh, aye, I have some contacts through the church that might be able to help me track her down," she said. "I'm always willing to play matchmaker."

Mary shook her head. "For some reason, I didn't think Sean's interest was romantic."

"When a man goes looking for a woman," Ian laughed. "It's always romantic. Unless, of course, she has him under a spell."

"Yes, that's what I'm afraid of," Mary said soberly.

Chapter Seven

The kindergarten play area, separated from the rest of the school playground, was nearly deserted, only Maggie and Clarissa sat on the swings, barely swinging in the cool spring morning. They both had their shoes partially buried in the sand and gave half-hearted pushes to keep the swings moving. "They really said they were going to kick you out when they had babies of their own?" Maggie asked, horror and disbelief warring on her face.

Sighing, Clarissa kicked at the ground again. "Well, not exactly," she admitted. "But you should have seen his face. He was so happy about Mary having babies. I know they're not going to want to have me around."

"But you're his own kid," Maggie argued. "Of course he wants you around."

Clarissa leaned her head against the swing's chain and blinked back the tears. "No, he told Mary that he would miss her, but he didn't say he'd miss me. He just said he'd see me later."

"That's just how dads talk," Maggie said. "He'll miss you too."

"What if he sends me away? What if he gives me up for adoption?" she asked. "No one wants me."

"Of course people want you, your mom and dad wanted you," Maggie said.

36

"They left me too," Clarissa responded with a spurt of anger. "Both of them left me. And Mrs. Gunderson said I was a stupid brat that no one would want once my mom died."

"Your mom and dad didn't leave you," Maggie said. "They died. It wasn't because of you."

"My dad died because of me," she countered. "He went to the bad man and told him to leave us alone, and the bad man killed him. I heard people talking about it. And if my dad wasn't dead, he would have taken care of my mom and she wouldn't be dead either."

Maggie shook her head, knowing her friend was wrong but not quite sure how to explain it. "You're wrong," she said, trying to come up with some way to show it. "And I can prove it."

"How?" Clarissa asked.

"Let's go back to your old house and see if your dad's ghost is still there," she said. "And we can ask him. He'll tell you the truth."

Clarissa lifted her head and stared at her friend. "Really?"

Maggie nodded. "Really."

Looking around at the school children starting to mill around the doors waiting for the entrance bell to ring, she jumped off her swing. "We have to go now before the teachers see us."

Maggie slid off her swing too. "Now? You mean skip school?" she replied. "I don't think that's a good idea."

"Come on, Maggie," Clarissa insisted. "It's important. Maybe if he's still there, I can live with him."

"We're going to get in trouble," Maggie said. "Bad trouble."

"We'll just tell them we got sick and were trying to go home but we got lost," Clarissa suggested.

Maggie looked at the school building and then looked back at her friend. Sighing, she hitched her backpack onto her shoulders and nodded. "Okay, we better hurry."

Rushing through the schoolyard, they ran past the line of children and ran out to the teacher's parking lot. Hiding between cars, they made their way to the street on the far side of the school. Secreted behind a van, they waited until the bell rang and the rest of the students entered the school. A few minutes later, the crossing guard slipped her bright orange vest off and walked over to her car. As soon as the car was out of sight, the girls ran out of the parking lot and crossed the street. "Do you remember where your house is?" Maggie asked.

Pausing and looking around for a moment, Clarissa nodded. "Yes, I remember my mom picking me up," she said. "It's only a few minutes away from here. Come on."

Clarissa started running up the street with Maggie following close behind. They stopped at the next corner and, after carefully looking both ways, they ran across the street and continued their pace.

Three blocks away from the school, Maggie tugged on Clarissa's backpack to stop her. "I have to tie my shoe," she panted. "We have to stop for a minute."

Looking around to be sure it was safe, Clarissa nodded. "Okay," she gasped. "You hide behind the tree and tie your shoe, and I'll look down the street to make sure we're safe."

Shrugging off her backpack, Maggie collapsed behind the tree and took her time tying her loose shoelace. Clarissa walked across the grass to the curb, slipped between two parked cars and peered down the street. Across the street, coming from the other direction, a car slowed and a window was rolled down. "Excuse me, little girl," the man in the driver's seat said. "Are you lost? Do you need a ride?"

Her heart pounding and eyes wide, she shook her head. "No, no, I'm fine," she stammered.

Stopping the car across from her, he looked up and down the street. "I don't see anyone with you," he said. "It's dangerous for a pretty young girl like you to be outside all alone."

"I'm not alone," she said, backing up. "My, um, my mom is just coming out of the house."

He quickly glanced up and looked around. "I don't see anyone coming at all," he said. "Why don't you let me give you a ride? I like pretty little girls."

Clarissa nearly screamed when Maggie came up behind her and pulled on her backpack. "He's a bad man," Maggie whispered urgently. "There are ghosts in his car with him. We have to run away, now!"

The girls turned and ran down the street.

"Wait!" the man called, jumping out of his car and running after them. "You come back here right now!"

Running as fast as they could, the girls ran toward the corner. "Hurry, Clarissa, hurry," Maggie urged, leading the way. "He's starting to come after us."

Clarissa looked up to see Maggie running into the intersection without looking. Then she saw the black car hurtling down the road. "Maggie, look out," she screamed, jumping forward and pulling hard on Maggie's backpack.

The car screeched to a halt, but Maggie was already careening toward Clarissa, sending them both backward onto the pavement.

"Are you okay?" the elderly woman asked, looking through the passenger side window.

Bruised and scraped, the girls nodded, and slowly got up. "I'm fine," Maggie said.

"Well, you need to watch where you're going," the old woman yelled. "I could have killed you."

"Yes, ma'am," Maggie replied, tears sliding down her cheeks. "I'm sorry."

"Why aren't you in school?" she asked. "Do I need to call the police?"

Clarissa shook her head. "No! No! Don't call the police," she said. "We...we missed our bus and we had to walk. That's why we're late."

The woman stared at them for a moment. "Alright, I won't call the police," she said. "But I'm going to follow you to the school and make sure you end up where you're supposed to be. I'm not going to offer you a ride because I know you're both too smart to get into a car with a stranger."

"Yes, ma'am," Clarissa agreed, looking over her shoulder to discover the man and his car were both gone.

"Good," the woman replied. "Now start walking."

Chapter Eight

Jamming the gear shift into reverse, he quickly sped backward down the street the moment he saw the old woman stop her car. They had been perfect, two little girls. He hadn't caught two together in a long time. He nearly had them, if he had only run a little faster.

He turned down the alley and drove to the side street, watching the girls walk toward the school, the dark car following them. There was no way he could capture them now. He leaned forward and studied them. They had been afraid, not just of him, but of being caught. He knew that look on their faces, guilt and fear combined. They weren't going to tell anyone about him because they would be incriminating themselves. *Besides*, he grinned, *what could they say?*

He took another look at them, especially the second one who had come out of nowhere. She was different. She looked past him, into his car and her eyes had widened. He glanced over his shoulder to the empty seat behind him. *What had she seen?*

Shaking his head, he pressed on the accelerator and turned the car down the street in the opposite direction of the school and the girls. He would be watching for them. If they tried to skip school once, he was sure they would try again. And this time, he would be more ready for them. *But now, he thought with a smile spreading across his face, I need to find the other students who have skipped school today and maybe, another special one will be out there for me to add to my collection.*

Chapter Nine

"Why aren't you in school?" Mike asked, appearing next to the girls as they walked down the street toward the school.

Clarissa and Maggie both jumped when he appeared. "Hey, something's got you spooked," he said. "What's up?"

An unspoken agreement passed between the girls before either one spoke. "You just scared us," Clarissa said. "Why did you come anyway?"

Mike shrugged, eyeing the two carefully. "My spidey-sense told me you were in trouble," he said. "What are you two up to?"

"Nothing," Maggie said, not meeting his eyes. "We just missed the bus, so we had to walk to school and we're late."

"Wait, you missed the bus and you didn't think either of your mothers would have driven you to school?" he asked. "Okay, that one is not going to fly."

"We didn't want to ask them," Clarissa said, "because we wanted an adventure."

"An adventure?" Mike asked. "That comes with skinned knees and cut hands? I don't think so."

"Don't tell on us, Mike," Maggie pleaded. "It was my fault. I wasn't looking when I crossed the street and a car was coming. Clarissa had to pull me back and the car slammed on its brakes."

"That's why the lady in the car is following us to school," Clarissa explained. "Because she wants to make sure we get there safely."

Mike turned and looked over his shoulder at the black car that was slowly following the girls. "Okay, that's creepy," Mike said.

"Not as creepy as the other car," Maggie blurted out.

"What other car?" Mike asked as Clarissa sent Maggie a look of exasperation.

"Oh, just a car we saw," Clarissa said. "It was really weird."

"Well, stay away from weird cars," he lectured. "And look both ways before you cross the street. Come on, you guys aren't little kids anymore, you should know better."

"Yes, Mike," Maggie said. "I'm sorry."

"Me too," Clarissa agreed. "We won't do this ever again."

Sighing, Mike walked along with them in silence for a few moments. He knew something was wrong, especially when he went into panic mode for a few minutes. He looked down at the girls, who seemed subdued but safe. Maybe it was just because Maggie had nearly been hit by the car. Perhaps he had just sensed Clarissa's fear. He sure wished he understood this whole angel thing better.

"Okay, I'm not going to mention this to either of your parents," Mike finally said. "I understand what it's like to be young and stupid. But no more adventures like this, do you promise?"

Clarissa stuck her hand behind her back and crossed her little fingers. "Promise," she replied as earnestly as she could.

Maggie looked at Clarissa, not seeing her crossed fingers, and nodded her head. "I promise too," she said.

They stopped in front of the school. The lady in the black car leaned out her window once more. "Now you get into that school and get to class right away," she said. "Understand?"

"Yes, ma'am," Maggie replied.

Clarissa nodded sincerely. "Yes, we will."

The black car sped down the street and the girls sighed with relief.

"You're not out of the woods yet," Mike said. "You still need to deal with your principal and with your parents if she decides to call them."

"Can't you just help us sneak in?" Clarissa asked, sending Mike a pleading look.

"Oh, sure, because that's what angels are all about, cheating and lying," Mike responded. "Not! You both need to accept responsibility for your actions. You made a bad choice and now you get to live with the consequences."

"But we don't want these consequences," Maggie complained.

Mike shrugged. "Well, then you shouldn't have made that choice."

He walked them up to the door, but as soon as they put their hands on the handle, the fire alarm began to sound. Clarissa looked up at Mike. "Hey, don't look at me. I didn't do it."

The girls stood back as the doors burst open and class after class hurried out. When their class exited, they moved in at the end of the line, as if they had always been with the group.

"Maggie, Clarissa," their teacher called, as she walked toward them.

The girls both held their breaths, waiting for the worst. "Yes?" Maggie asked.

"I thought I told everyone to leave their backpacks in the classroom," she said. "In an emergency the only thing that's important is to get to safety. Your personal belongings do not matter."

"I'm sorry," Clarissa said. "We didn't hear you."

"Well, next time I don't want to see those backpacks."

"Yes, ma'am," Maggie replied.

When their teacher hurried away to deal with two boys who were shoving each other, the girls once again breathed a sigh of relief. "Even though you both got off way too easy," Mike said. "I hope you've learned your lesson."

Clarissa nodded. "Yes, Mike, we have."

Maggie agreed. "We'll never do this again," she said. "We promised."

The return bell sounded over the loudspeakers in the playground.

"Looks like you just got the all clear," Mike said. "Now behave yourselves."

As soon as Mike disappeared, Clarissa turned to Maggie. "Next time we go, we're going to have to figure out a better plan."

"Next time?" Maggie replied, astonished. "We promised we would never do this again. We promised to an angel."

Shaking her head, Clarissa smiled and lifted her hand with her crossed fingers. "I had my fingers crossed," she said. "So I didn't promise."

"Well, I did," Maggie countered. "So we can't go!"

"You can't go," Clarissa argued. "I still can."

"Clarissa, we almost had a stranger take us. It's not safe."

"He didn't almost get us. We got away," she said. "Besides, we'll never see him again."

"I'm not going," Maggie stated firmly.

"I'll just go without you then," Clarissa countered.

"But you can't see if your dad is there without me," Maggie said.

Clarissa stared at Maggie for a moment, her lips tight and her hands clenched in fists. "If you don't come, I'll never be your friend again," she shouted, turning and hurrying toward the school door without Maggie.

Maggie stood alone for a moment, remembering the ghosts inside the man's car. All of them were pounding on the windows, tears flowing from their eyes and pleading with Maggie to help them escape. She was more afraid than she had ever been. That man was too dangerous. "Clarissa, wait," Maggie called, moving after her. "You have to listen to me."

Chapter Ten

Mary unlocked the door to her office, walked in and looked around with a look of satisfaction on her face. She couldn't imagine life getting any better than it was. She had a wonderful career, an amazing husband who adored her and a new daughter who was nearly perfect. And now, with the drama and worry of the past months over, she could finally just live her life.

Walking to her desk, she put her briefcase down and slipped out of her coat. A quick knock on the door had her turning around and smiling. Stanley was strolling through the front door with a white paper box in his hands. Her smile widened as she saw the familiar logo of Coles' Bakery.

"So, girlie, you interested in one of these chocolate éclairs?" he asked with a twinkle in his eye.

"I really shouldn't," she said.

"Yeah, but you want to," he coaxed.

"I really do," she confessed. "And for some reason, I'm just starving today."

Walking to her desk, he sat on one of the chairs and put the box down. "Well, you know, you've been through a lot of changes in your life lately," he said, as he untied the twine that kept the box closed. "And that causes stress. And that burns up calories. And that makes you hungry."

He reached in, pulled out a six-inch éclair loaded with whipped filling and covered with dark chocolate and handed it to her. "And that's why you need to eat this."

Mary took a bite and closed her eyes in bliss as the flaky pastry, smooth cream and dark chocolate slid over her taste buds and down her throat. "Oh, Stanley," she said, "this is just heavenly."

Stanley lifted the other one out of the box and took a bite. "Yeah, it ain't too bad, is it?" he asked through a mouthful of pastry. "Wonder if Rosie can make these?"

Mary took another bite and wiped the excess filling from her chin. "So, why isn't Rosie baking these for you?" she asked. "I'd bet you haven't stepped through the doorway of Coles' since you got married."

Nodding, as he took another bite, he swallowed before he answered. "Rosie's got some important real estate seminar in Chicago," he said. "So, I'm by myself for a couple of days."

"Do you want to come over for dinner tonight?" she asked, licking the frosting from her fingers.

Wiping his face with a paper napkin, he shook his head as he stood up. "Naw, this is your first night as a normal family," he said. "You need to be alone. 'Sides, Rosie cooked me up a bunch of casseroles and iffen I don't eat them, she'll be put out."

Mary picked up another napkin, sat back in her chair and wiped the traces of the treat off her face too. "It's nice to have someone worry about you, isn't it?" she asked.

He smiled down at her. "We done good, you and me," he said. "We found soul mates. Not everyone gets that."

"Yes, you're right," she agreed, sighing with satisfaction. "And we get to live happily ever after."

Stanley chortled. "Girlie, you've read too many of those fairy tales," he said. "You want to know why they always end the story right after the prince and the princess gets married?"

"Why?" she asked.

"'Cause the rest of their lives is just plain ugly," he said.

"Stanley!" she scolded. "I can't believe you said that. Being married to Rosie isn't ugly."

"I ain't saying it is," he said. "But the being married part, the putting two people together and trying to act like one, the making of a good marriage – it ain't purty. It's like making sausage; it's ugly, but it's worth it."

Crossing her arms, she shook her head. "I think you're pretty cynical," she said.

"Nope, just realistic," he replied. "After the twitterpated part wears off, you start seeing stuff that you didn't pay attention to before."

"Stuff?"

"Like he always leaves the top off the toothpaste and doesn't clean up after himself in the bathroom," he suggested, his right eyebrow lifting toward his forehead.

"Okay, well, yes, he might do that," she said. "But I just think it's cute."

"'Course you do, you're still twitterpated," he replied. "But when that first goofy love settles down to a real, deep love, then you start looking at him like a partner and things start bugging you."

Worried, she sat forward and placed her head on her hands. "Bugging me?"

"Yeah, and bugging him too," he said.

"There is nothing about me that would bug Bradley," she said instantly. "He loves me too much."

"Now there you go, girlie, mistaking love for human nature," he said. "'Course he loves you. 'Course he'd die for you. 'Course you're the only woman for him. But you're a woman and he's a man; you don't think the same way and you don't act the same way. There's gonna be some bumps in the road."

"So, what do I do?" she asked.

"You gotta remember he don't think like you and he don't see stuff the way you do," he said, his voice softening as he spoke. "You just gotta talk to him when something hurts your feelings. Let him know how you feel. Don't get angry with him for being a man, he can't help that, but explain to him how you're feeling about things."

She plopped back against her chair. "So, there is no happily-ever-after?"

Stanley reached forward and patted her hand. "Sure there is, girlie," he said. "It just don't happen by itself. It takes two people working hard together, respecting each other and thinking about the other person first – that makes it happen."

"I can do that," she said hopefully.

"If anyone can do that, you can," Stanley replied with confidence as he stood up. "Now, I gotta go to the store and make sure those youngsters are keeping busy."

Mary smiled, picturing the fifty-year-old youngsters Stanley was referring to. "Don't let them get away with lollygagging," she laughed.

Winking at her, he stopped at the door before leaving. "Don't worry, you got lots of time 'fore the twitterpated part ends. Lots of time."

Chapter Eleven

A few minutes after Stanley left, Mary heard the bell jingle again. She looked up to see a woman enter the office.

"Hi, can I help you?" Mary asked, standing and walking around her desk.

Hesitant, the woman took a deep breath and finally nodded. "My name is Celia Rasmussen and I hope you can help me."

Quickly assessing the woman, Mary decided she was probably in her late forties, but she was carrying a burden that made her seem older. She looked exhausted, but Mary could tell it was a chronic fatigue that had lasted many years. She wondered if the woman was sick.

"Hello, Mrs. Rasmussen," she said, guiding her to a chair next to her desk. "Please, have a seat. What can I do for you?"

Moving to the other side of the desk, she sat in her chair, her expression patient and open, and waited.

"I feel like I've given up by coming to you," Celia said bluntly.

"Given up?" Mary asked. "In what way?"

"Eight years ago my daughter was kidnapped," Celia explained. "There were no clues, no explanations, no leads, and we never found her."

"I am so sorry," Mary said.

Acknowledging Mary's comment with a nod, she picked up the manila folder she had on her lap and handed it to her. Mary opened the file and saw a printout of a pixelated photo. "What am I looking for?" she asked.

Celia stood up and leaned over the desk, pointing to a small area in the photo where brush and trees overlapped. "See. In here," she said, indicating a deviation in the colors of the leaves. "If you look closely, you can see Courtney's face."

Mary pulled a magnifying glass out of her desk drawer and studied the photo. There was a difference in the photo that had nothing to do with sunlight and shade. There seemed to be a girl's face in the midst of the trees. "When was this taken?" she asked.

"Last week," Celia said, "during a softball tournament at the park. It was in the background of the shot, that's why it's so blurry. But it's Courtney, I can tell."

"I have to be honest and tell you this photo is so pixelated it's hard to tell what this is, let alone pick out features," Mary began. "I don't know…"

"A mother knows her own daughter," Celia interrupted. "Do you think I would mistake my own daughter?"

It only took Mary a moment to respond. "No, I don't think you would," she agreed. "I think a mother's intuition is one of the strongest forces on earth."

Breathing a sigh of relief, Celia sat back in her chair. "Thank you," she said.

"But why haven't you brought this to the police?" Mary asked.

"Because they don't have time or resources to deal with fairly vague leads on an eight-year-old case," she said openly. "I don't blame them; I just have to look for other options."

Picking up the magnifying glass again, Mary peered back down at the photo. The shot was so bad it looked like you could see through the face to the trees behind her. As soon as that thought went through her head, she froze and looked up at Celia.

"Why did you choose me for your option?" Mary asked softly.

Celia swallowed and took a deep shuddering breath. "I think you know," she said, meeting Mary's eyes directly. "But I'm afraid…"

Laying the magnifying glass to the side of the desk, Mary met the woman's eyes. "Now, I need to tell you a little bit about myself before we continue."

"Okay," Celia replied hesitantly.

"I used to work for the Chicago Police Department and during that time I was shot in the line of duty."

"Oh, that must have been horrible for you," Celia gasped. "Were you hurt badly?"

"I died," Mary said. "And then I had the most unusual conversation. I was told that I had a choice: I could continue on to the light, or I could come back

57

and be with my friends and family. Only this time, my time on earth would be different."

"Different? In what way?" Celia asked.

"Different because now I can see and communicate with ghosts," Mary replied softly.

"Most people think there are no such things as ghosts," Celia said, a flicker of hope glowing in her eyes. "People don't believe in ghosts."

Mary shrugged. "That's true," she said. "Many people don't believe in ghosts until they have an encounter of their very own and that somehow, quickly, changes their mind."

"They say ghosts are evil," she said. "Do you believe that?"

"Ghosts are just people who died," Mary explained. "They are as good or evil as they were as people. For some reason, they haven't passed over to the other side. That's part of my calling – I get to help those people figure out what's keeping them here and help them pass over."

Celia was quiet for a moment and then tears filled her eyes. "I think I've seen her," she whispered hoarsely.

Mary nodded but didn't say a word.

"Out of the corner of my eye," Celia continued, "I'll see her running up the stairs or walking through the kitchen. Of course, when I turn to look, she's never there."

Mary picked up a pen and jotted down a few notes. "When do you see her?"

Celia shrugged. "The first time was on Mother's Day, a few weeks after she disappeared," she admitted. "I just thought it was because I wanted to see her."

"But then?" Mary prompted.

"But then I would see her in places I didn't expect," she explained. "I mean, if I was imagining her, wouldn't I kind of be expecting her?"

"Seems like that would make sense," Mary agreed. "So, what do you think?"

A soft sob escaped through her lips and a moment later she was bent forward, weeping uncontrollably, her head pillowed in her arms. "My baby," she cried. "I think my baby's dead."

Mary grabbed the box of tissues on her desk and came around, crouching next to Celia. She put her arms around the woman and just let her continue to cry for a few more minutes. Finally, the crying calmed and Celia pulled away. Mary handed her the tissue box, but stayed close to her.

"What would you like me to do for you?" she asked softly.

Wiping the moisture from her face, Celia looked up at her, her face red and blotchy, her mascara smeared down her cheeks. "I want you to find her," she whispered. "And I want you to find the man who did this to her. I want him to pay. I want him to never be able to do this to another child."

Mary nodded. "Do you want to help me?" she asked, making a quick decision.

Celia's eyes widened. "What do you mean?" she asked, a slight edge of hope in her voice.

"Do you want to help me investigate this crime?" Mary asked. "I think we could work well together."

Taking a deep breath, Celia nodded. "I would like that."

"Okay, meet me here tomorrow morning at nine and we'll start," she said.

"I'll be here," Celia agreed.

"Oh, and if you could jot down anything you can remember about Courtney's visits, that would be helpful."

Celia started to stand, and then stopped. "So, I'm not crazy?"

Mary smiled. "No more crazy than me," she said.

Chapter Twelve

Bradley leaned over and pushed the intercom button for the tenth time in two hours. "Sorry, Dorothy," he said. "But I can't seem to find the file containing the minutes from the last city council meeting."

"Oh, the mayor didn't send them over to you," she replied. "He told his secretary, who told me, that if you couldn't find the time in your busy schedule to make the meetings, you probably didn't have time to read the minutes."

Taking a deep breath and counting to ten, he waited before responding. "Did you mention to his secretary that I was on my honeymoon?" he asked.

"Yes, I did," she replied. "And I also mentioned that this was the first vacation you had taken in the two years you have held the position."

Touched by her loyalty, Bradley felt an easing in his chest. "Thank you, Dorothy," he said.

"And I told her if the mayor wasn't such a complete idiot, he would have been invited to the wedding and he would have known about it firsthand," she finished.

Bradley dropped his head into his hand. "You really didn't say that, did you?" he asked.

He heard her chuckle softly. "No, I didn't," she replied. "But it went through my mind."

His sigh of relief was audible. "Okay, well, is there any way you can get me a copy of those minutes?" he asked. "Or do I have to walk over to the mayor's office and beg for them?"

"They will be on your desk in ten minutes," she replied defiantly.

"Thanks, Dorothy," he said, a slight smile forming on his lips. "Oh, and Dorothy…"

"Yes?"

"Try not to get us fired."

She laughed. "Yes, sir," she replied.

He hung up the phone, sat back in his chair and rubbed his temples, trying to ease the headache that had been growing steadily all day. He couldn't believe the backlog on his desk from being away for only two weeks. The city, county and state reports alone were going to keep him working until at least ten o'clock tonight. Good thing he and Mary hadn't planned anything special.

The phone rang and he rolled his eyes before picking it up. "What now?" he asked, before announcing into the phone, "Chief Alden."

"Mary O'Reilly Alden," Mary responded, a smile in her voice.

The tension in his body eased and a real smile formed on his face. "Hi."

"Hi yourself, how's your day going?"

"Don't ask," he said.

"That bad, huh?" she replied. "Well, will it make you feel better to know I've picked up some ribeye steaks for dinner tonight?"

He groaned silently. "About dinner," he said. "I'm going to have to take a raincheck on those ribeyes. I'm going to be here until late tonight."

"But it's our first dinner together as a family," she replied, disappointment evident in her voice.

That's strange, Bradley thought, *she must have forgotten we ate dinner last night together.*

"No it's not," he said, trying to gently remind her. "We ate dinner last night as a family, remember?"

"But we had just gotten home," she argued. "We hadn't been together for the whole day."

Shaking his head, Bradley replied quickly. "But we aren't going to be together for the whole day today either," he said. "You and I are at work and Clarissa's at school. So, really, it's no big deal."

Mary's heart dropped. She had wanted to create a special meal just for the three of them. A symbol that would set the pattern for their lives together. How could he not see that it was, indeed, a very big deal?

"But Bradley," she began and then she heard his other line ringing.

"I'm sorry, sweetheart," he interrupted her. "I've got to take this other call. Love you. See you later tonight."

He hung up the phone before she could respond.

"Chief Alden," he said, answering the other line and then he closed his eyes and grimaced as he heard the voice on the other end of the line. "Yes, sir,

I would consider it a personal favor. Yes, I certainly won't make a habit of missing the city council meetings. Thank you."

He hung up the phone and immediately turned to his computer, bringing up a new email and adding Mary's address. He was just about to send her a quick note apologizing for missing their dinner and explaining about his day when the phone rang again. "Chief Alden," he replied, and tucking the phone between his shoulder and his cheek, his fingers paused over the keyboard.

He stopped typing and turned back to his desk, pulling a notepad across the desk. "How long has she been missing?" he asked, jotting notes down quickly. "What's her address? Are both of her parents there? Okay, I'll be there in five minutes."

He pushed away from the desk, pulled on his jacket and hat, and hurried out of his office. "Dorothy," he said as he passed his assistant in the hallway. "We've got a missing child. I'm heading over to interview her parents."

Nodding, she waved the manila folder in her hand at him. "These will be waiting for you on your desk when you get back," she said. "Good luck."

"Thanks," he replied. "Let's pray we can find this one."

Chapter Thirteen

On the bus ride home, Clarissa and Maggie sat silently for the first few minutes, neither girl wanting to break the silence first. Finally Maggie couldn't stand it. "The man in the car was really bad," she said. "There were ghosts in his car, ghosts that were crying and wanted to get out."

Clarissa felt a cold shiver move up her spine. "Like he took them?" she asked quietly.

Maggie nodded. "Like he took them and they never went home," she replied.

Swallowing softly, Clarissa turned to Maggie. "He wanted to take us," she said. "Didn't he?"

"I think so," Maggie answered. "And I don't think he was happy that we escaped. I bet he's worried that we're going to tell someone about him."

"We can't," Clarissa said, shaking her head excitedly. "Then for sure Mary and Bradley won't want me."

Maggie plopped back against the seat and turned to Clarissa. "I can't believe they wouldn't want you," she said. "They love you. They saved you from the bad man. They were looking for you."

"But now they want their own babies," she argued. "Like Mrs. Gunderson said, no one wants me. I'm just trouble. And if we tell them, I'll be even more trouble."

"We should tell Mike," Maggie said. "If we can't tell Mary and Bradley, Mike would be able to help us."

"But remember what he said on the playground," she said. "He can't help us lie, so he'd have to tell them too. 'Sides, he told us we had to deal with our own consequences."

Sighing, Maggie thought about Clarissa's words for a few moments. "He did say that," she agreed. "But I don't think he meant dangerous things."

"Maybe my dad can help," Clarissa suggested.

"Bradley?" Maggie asked hopefully.

"No, my 'doptive dad," she said. "He protected me from the bad man when he was alive. Maybe he can help us with this too."

"I don't think that's a good idea," Maggie said. "And maybe your dad isn't there anymore. Maybe he passed over, just like your mom."

A tear slipped down Clarissa's cheek and she brushed it away. "So, you think no one wants me?" she asked sadly. "You think everyone left me alone?"

Her little heart breaking, Maggie shook her head and leaned over to her friend. "No. No, of course not," she said. "But they knew you were in good hands. They knew Mary and Bradley were going to take care of you and love you. That's why they could go."

Clarissa's lower lip quivered with emotion and she took a deep shaky breath. "But they don't want me," she replied. "I tried and tried to do everything I thought they wanted, but all Bradley wants is a new baby."

"We could talk to my mom," Maggie suggested. "She would know how to fix this."

"No," Clarissa replied adamantly. "She'd just tell me I was silly. She'd tell Mary and Bradley, and they would get angry. Please, Maggie, promise me you won't tell her."

Sighing, Maggie nodded. "I won't tell her," she said. "But we've got to tell someone."

"That's why we need to talk to my dad," Clarissa explained. "He knows stuff."

"And if he tells us to talk to Mary and Bradley?" Maggie countered.

Clarissa hesitated for a moment and then nodded. "If he says to talk to them, I will," she agreed.

Maggie sat back in her chair and folded her arms across her chest. "Okay, we can go and try to find him," she agreed. "But we have to do it so we don't get in trouble."

"How about next week?" Clarissa suggested. "We have a half-day on Tuesday. We could go then."

Nodding slowly as she thought about it, Maggie suddenly smiled. "You can tell Mary and Bradley that you're coming to my house and I can tell my mom that I'm going to your house," she said. "Then we can do whatever we want to do."

"Great!" Clarissa said. "I'll tell them tonight."

Maggie rolled her eyes. "You're not very good at this, are you?"

"What?" Clarissa asked.

"You don't tell them until the day you want to go," she replied. "That way they can't check with each other."

"Oh," Clarissa replied.

"And you ask them when they are busy with something else, so they really aren't paying attention to you," Maggie added.

"Does that really work for you?" Clarissa asked.

Grinning, Maggie nodded. "All the time," she said. "All the time."

Chapter Fourteen

Mary arrived home only moments before the bus pulled up to the curb. She hurried to the front porch to greet Clarissa, worried about the way things had gone that morning. After waving to Maggie and her brothers as they exited the bus and walked toward their house, she turned to watch Clarissa slowly exit the bus, her head down, and walk toward the house.

"Hello sweetheart," Mary said. "How was school today?"

"Fine," Clarissa replied softly.

"I picked up some wonderful things for dinner tonight," she continued, trying to make conversation. "I thought it would be lovely to have a special dinner, just you and me."

Clarissa froze and looked up at her. "Bradley...I mean, Dad's not coming home?" she asked.

Mary shook her head, trying to keep the disappointment from her face. "No," she said brightly. "He has to stay and do some extra work at the office. So, it's just us girls. Won't that be fun?"

Sighing loudly, Clarissa nodded. "I have lots of homework," she announced. "So, I won't be in your way."

"Clarissa," Mary replied, nearly dumbstruck by Clarissa's remark. "You are never in my way. Never think that."

"Okay," Clarissa replied meekly. "I won't."

She scooted around Mary and made her way into the house. Hanging her coat in the closet, she turned to start up the stairs.

"Don't you want an afterschool treat?" Mary asked.

Halting on the steps, Clarissa turned back. "You don't have to bother," she said.

"Darling, it's no bother," Mary answered, moving into the kitchen and pulling the peanut butter and bread from the cabinet. "I could make you a sandwich with some milk. How does peanut butter and jelly sound?"

Shaking her head, Clarissa started up the stairs again. "It's okay, I can wait until dinner."

Mary watched her slowly walk up the stairs and waited until she heard the door close to Clarissa's bedroom. She pulled out a piece of bread, slathered it liberally with peanut butter, folded it and took a big bite. "So much for happily ever after," she muttered.

"Sorry, I couldn't understand you," Mike said from behind her. "Your mouth was full."

Startled, Mary jumped and then turned on her friend. "I feel like I've walked away from my life and into an episode of the Twilight Zone," she said, taking her frustration out on the sandwich with an angry bite.

"Wow. Remind me to never get close to your choppers when you're angry," he teased.

"It's just that…" she started. "It's just that…"

Suddenly, tears began to flow down her cheeks and she felt overwhelmed. She sank down into the nearest chair, next to the table, and laid her head in her arms and cried.

"Hey, now, it can't be that bad," Mike said, floating over next to her.

"It is," she said, her voice muffled by her arms. "It's terrible."

"What's terrible?" he asked.

"Bradley can't be home for dinner," she muttered through the peanut butter.

Mike leaned closer to hear her. "Bradley can't be a humdinger?" Mike asked. "Well, babe, not everyone can be like me."

She shook her head. "No, he's not coming home," she said emphatically.

"What? When did this happen?" he exclaimed. "What the…heck? Is he abandoning you and Clarissa?"

Lifting her head, Mary reached for a tissue, blew her nose and wiped her eyes. "No, he's not abandoning us," she said. "He can't make it home for dinner."

Mike exhaled in relief. "Well, if that's all," he began.

"All?" Mary exclaimed, slapping her hands against the table. "Is that all? On our first night together as a family, for our first real family meal, he decides to work late."

Mike nodded and sat in a seat across from Mary. "What an idiot," he said, agreeing with Mary. "I mean, really, what's so important about his job that he can't come home for dinner? Before you were married he never had to cancel. Oh, no, he's just doing this to make you angry."

She started to agree, but snapped her mouth closed for a moment. "Okay, yes, his job has always made him late for dinner," she confessed.

"Well, yes, maybe," Mike said. "But if he really wanted to be here, he'd be here."

Once again, she tried to agree with him, and then shook her head. "No, I could tell, even though he was distracted, he wanted to be here."

"Well, yes, but…" Mike began.

"Mike," Mary interrupted, a wry smile on her face.

"Yes, Mary," he replied with a grin.

"I get your point. You can stop now."

"See, I told everyone you weren't slow," he chuckled.

She sat back against the kitchen chair and sighed. "It's just…it's just…" she started.

"It's just not how you pictured it," Mike inserted.

She turned to him and nodded emphatically. "Yes. Yes, that's it exactly," she agreed. "It's not how I pictured it."

"So, what are you going to do about it?" he asked.

"Change the picture I guess," she decided. "Dinner together is great, but maybe breakfast would be more realistic."

"That's my girl," he replied.

She nodded and smiled. "I mean, really, there's no reason to miss breakfast."

"It's the most important meal of the day," Mike agreed.

"Thanks, Mike. Now everything is going to be perfect."

Chapter Fifteen

Bradley winced when the front door squeaked as he opened it sometime around midnight that night. He had followed up on some leads on the missing girl, had spoken at length with her distraught parents and worked with the local FBI office to fill them in on the pertinent information. He was exhausted, but he was also so wound up he knew he wouldn't be able to fall asleep right away. He kept seeing the face of the girl; in many ways she reminded him of Clarissa. His heart broke for her parents because he couldn't imagine what he would do if his daughter was missing.

He quietly laid his coat over the back of the closest chair and put his gun in the safe in the closet. He was about to flip open his laptop and work a little longer when his stomach growled, and he realized he hadn't eaten anything since he had grabbed a quick sandwich at lunch.

Walking into the kitchen, he wondered if he would have to settle for peanut butter and jelly. But when he opened the refrigerator, he found a plate of food already made for him, with a yellow sticky note that had a heart drawn on it.

Mary. His burden suddenly seemed a little lighter. Pulling out the plate, he noticed a tray filled with white ramekins, the kind Mary used when she made stuffed French toast. His smile widened. *Being married is great.*

Carrying his food into the living room, he turned his favorite cable news station on low and flipped open his laptop, sharing his time between both as he ate his food. The FBI reports on the missing girl were linked to some older cases in Stephenson County. He clicked on the oldest one as he bit into the steak sandwich. *Courtney Rasmussen,* he mused, *she was one of the first.*

The agent from the Rockford office had been very helpful, but Bradley was a little chagrined to discover in the past ten years they had had an epidemic of missing children cases in the area. He knew their computer software wasn't compatible with neighboring towns and with the county, but there had to be some way they could all share data.

He yawned widely and stretched. Kicking off his shoes, he decided to just stretch out on the couch for a few minutes, and then he'd have the energy to go upstairs and get ready for bed. He closed his eyes and the world around him disappeared.

Chapter Sixteen

The room was dark and Mary was trying to understand why she was there. She moved forward tentatively, trying to find an exit door or a light. She didn't feel afraid, but she knew she didn't really belong there. A low sound, like the thrum of a bass note, was pulsing in the background, over some hidden speaker system. Everywhere she went, the sound was present. She continued forward and heard another sound, soft and whispered, in the distance. The sound of a child's cry. Dismissing caution, she hurried forward toward the source of the sound, running down dark corridors that turned and twisted. Finding herself at a dead end, she turned back and found a staircase that hadn't been there before. She jogged up stairs and down stairs, still following the elusive cry.

The alarm went off at six o'clock. Still half asleep, Mary jumped up, still searching for the child. Realizing it had only been a dream, she turned, seeking comfort in Bradley's arms. But her eyes widened and she was at full alert when she realized that not only wasn't he there, but his side of the bed hadn't been used the night before. *Did something happen to him at work? Has he been shot? Surely someone would have called me! What if my phone wasn't working? What if no one knows? What if he had been ambushed on the way home?*

Leaping from her bed, her heart in her throat, she grabbed her robe and rushed out of her room. She turned too quickly next to the staircase and rammed her toe into the post. Biting on her lip to keep from yelling in pain, she hobbled down the stairs.

She could hear the soft tones of the news station before she reached the first floor. The living room was still dark, but the glow of the television lit it enough for her to see that Bradley was stretched out on the couch, snoring slightly. She quietly moved closer and saw the remnants of his meal still on the coffee table in front of him. His clothes were rumpled and his shoes were laying on the floor right below his feet, as if he had kicked them off at the last moment.

Really? she thought. *You couldn't have just walked up the stairs and come to bed? Instead you decide to give me a heart attack the first thing in the morning.*

A part of her knew she was being unreasonable. A part of her realized he looked worn out. A part of her even had sympathy for the man slumbering on the couch. But another part of her was still reacting to her initial panic and her throbbing toe. And that part was really angry.

Taking a deep breath, she stepped away from him. *I'll just go up, shower and get dressed, and then I'll make breakfast. And when he wakes up, we can talk about our schedules.*

No sooner had Mary walked upstairs and closed her bedroom door than Bradley's phone began to ring. Groggily, he reached into his pocket and brought the device to his ear, his eyes still closed. "Alden," he said roughly into the mouthpiece.

Slowly his eyes opened and he sat up on the couch. "Yeah, really?" he said, becoming more alert. "Don't the FBI ever sleep?"

He rubbed his face with his hand, wiping away the sleep and then ran it through his hair. "No, hey, it's not your fault," he said. "I got a couple of good hours of sleep. I'm good, really. And the sooner we can get them working on this case, the better."

He slowly looked around, saw the television was still on and the rest of the first floor was empty. "It looks like Mary and Clarissa are still asleep," he said. "So I'll come in right now, shower at the office and change into my extra uniform. Yeah, I can be there in ten minutes, so you can brief me before the seven o'clock meeting."

Stretching and trying to work the kinks out of his back, he finally reached over and slipped his shoes back on his feet. *I probably should leave Mary a note*, he thought.

He walked over to the desk and picked up a pen when his phone rang for a second time. "Chief Alden," he answered, dropping the pen. "Oh, traffic was better than you thought? Well, isn't that great. Yeah, sure, we can move the meeting up to six-thirty. No problem. I'm heading in right now."

Well, crap, it sure feels like this is going to be one of those days, he thought as he picked up his gear and hurried out of the house, closing the door softly behind him. *I'll just call Mary later, she'll understand.*

Mary heard the click of the door as she exited her bedroom. *No,* she thought, hurrying down the hall to the stairs, *he wouldn't just leave.*

Rushing down the stairs, she froze on the bottom step and looked into the living room. Bradley was no longer stretched out on the couch, his shoes were no longer on the floor and his coat was no longer on the back of the chair. She sat down on the steps, put her head in her hands and sighed. "Well, I guess the honeymoon is now officially over."

Chapter Seventeen

The young girl lifted her head from the bed and gazed around the small room. Everything around her seemed fuzzy, and her head felt like it was in a fog. Somewhere deep inside of her someone was screaming for her to run away, but she couldn't get her body to respond to the command. A door opened and bright light entered the dim room. She squinted, but didn't look away.

"Well, good morning. You're finally awake," the man's voice seemed to echo in the room and through her head. "Don't worry; sooner or later I'll get the portion right. I don't want to give you too little because we don't want you running away, do we? And we don't want to give you too much because then you could die, and we're not ready for that just yet, are we?"

Her hair was yanked and she collapsed against the bed, her head bent back. She gagged as the medicine was forced down her throat, and although she tried to move her face, it was caught in the iron grip of his hand.

"Now swallow it all up," he said. "That's a good girl."

He stroked her hair and her face. "Just relax," he said. "Just relax and everything will be just fine."

She whimpered softly. "Mommy," she whispered.

"Oh, honey, your mommy can't help you now," he said. "You've fallen down into the monster's lair and there's nothing anyone can do for you."

"Please," she begged.

"Look at the photos on the wall," he said, pointing to a collection of framed photographs. "Each of those girls was where you are now. And each of those girls learned what happens when you skip school. Then they all graduated. And you'll graduate too. Once I'm done with you."

"I don't want to die," she pleaded.

"I didn't say nothing about dying," he said. "I said you'd graduate, just like you would have if you hadn't decided to skip school. But don't worry, if you're nice to me, I'll let you stay down here with me for an entire school year."

He stroked her again. "Now, you just sit back and let that medicine kick in. Then we'll play some fun games before I have to go to work."

He tightened the strap that held her to the bed. "I'm just going upstairs to get ready, but don't you worry, I'll be back."

Chapter Eighteen

"I've spent last night getting to know you," Celia said as she entered Mary's office.

"I beg your pardon?" Mary replied.

Smiling, Celia slipped off her coat and hung it on the coatrack near the door. "I did some Internet research on you last night," she explained.

Sitting back in her chair, Mary pushed slightly away from the desk, took a sip of her Diet Pepsi and nodded. "Did you learn anything interesting?"

Celia nodded. "Yes, actually, I did. It's amazing how much you've done with your gift."

"I didn't realize I was even on the Internet."

"Not only in the news, but there are a lot of discussions about you on forums, especially paranormal forums," Celia added. "Some of it's quite fantastic and some isn't very flattering."

"Well, you can't believe everything you read," Mary replied with a smile.

Studying the woman in front of her, Celia wondered if she was indeed some miraculous psychic who was led by spirit helpers to solve murder cases or, on the other hand, if she was the crackpot detective wannabe that others on a few Internet forums suggested.

"Which should I believe?" Celia asked.

Laughing quietly, Mary nodded. "Good question. I think the best answer to that is that you need to determine for yourself who I am and if I'm crazy or not," she said with a self-depreciating smile. "I'm fine if you want to reserve judgment for a little while. Work with me, but hold back if you need to."

"So, what is it like?" Celia asked unexpectedly.

"What is what like?" Mary asked, a little confused at this turn in the conversation.

"Dying."

Taking a deep breath, Mary nodded slowly and put her soft drink on the desk. "Getting right to the heart of the matter, so to speak; that's fair."

Sitting forward in her chair, she placed her elbows on her desk and rested her head on her hands, meeting Celia's eyes directly. "Well, the getting shot part is not something I'd recommend. But the going to the light part is…" She paused for a moment, looking down at the desk, trying to find the right words. "It's like having amnesia. You forget about any problems or worries; you're just free and walking toward something you know is going to be great. You have this amazing sense of tranquility and peace…and there's also a familiarity about it. Like you're finally going home."

Mary looked up to find Celia's eyes filled with tears. "And then?" Celia prompted; her voice thick with emotion.

"Well, for me, that's where it ended," Mary explained. "I was given a choice and I chose to return, and I suppose you know the rest of the story."

"And you've been working with ghosts ever since?"

"No, I've been working with people ever since," Mary replied. "It just so happens that some of them are dead."

Celia smiled. "I like that; it makes them seem less scary."

"When you get the chance to know them, most of them aren't scary at all," she said. "They just need some help finding their way back home."

Pulling out a tissue and blotting her eyes, Celia nodded. "So, what should we do first?"

Mary smiled. It seemed that Celia had already made her up her mind about her. She moved a folder to the middle of her desk and opened it. "The first question I have is about other cases that are similar to Courtney's case," she said. "If there have been other disappearances, perhaps we can link things together and see if there are any connections."

Pulling out her own folder, Celia opened it and pushed it across the desk toward Mary. "Although the police haven't made any connections," she said, "I've been doing research on missing children, especially girls, in the area and I've found quite a few that I think match the profile."

Mary flipped through the newspaper articles from the various small towns in the areas and the Amber Alert press releases attached to the articles.

"Why don't the police believe these are connected?" she asked.

Celia sighed. "Well, to be fair, I've never shown these to the new police chief," she admitted. "But the former police chief didn't seem to have any interest in these cases because they were in other smaller towns in the county. And we don't have a database that links one jurisdiction to the other, so the connections might get overlooked."

"But what about the FBI? Wouldn't they have linked the disappearances?" Mary asked.

Shrugging, Celia sat back in her chair. "It could have been that they were far enough apart from each other that the connections weren't made," she said. "And it didn't help that the police department had to install a brand new computer system four years ago. A lot of the cases never got transitioned to the new system."

"So there might be other cases, older cases, that relate to Courtney's case?" she asked.

"Yes, I suppose so," Celia said. "But we have to go into the archives to get them."

Standing up and putting the files into her briefcase, Mary was ready for action. "Let's go down to City Hall and get access," she said.

"But how are we going to get permission?" Celia asked.

Mary smiled. "Let me worry about that," she replied. "I know a guy who owes me."

Chapter Nineteen

The preschool playground was empty, so Maggie and Clarissa hurried to the swing set as soon as they were released for recess. Through an unspoken agreement, neither child said anything until they had seated themselves on adjacent swings and set them barely moving.

"So, what happened last night?" Maggie asked. "Did Mike tell on you?"

Shaking her head, Clarissa smiled at her friend. "No, he just checked on me before I said my prayers and asked me if I had learned my lesson," she replied.

"So, what did you say?"

"I told him I learned my lesson really well," she said with a grin. "But he doesn't know the lesson was not to get caught."

Maggie didn't laugh. "I'm still worried about that man," she said. "I think we need to tell someone."

Clarissa swung in silence for the next few moments. "Bradley didn't come home last night," she said quietly.

"What?"

"He didn't come home from work," Clarissa replied. "It's already starting. He doesn't want to spend time with me."

Skidding her swing to a stop, Maggie turned to her friend. "I just can't believe that," she said. "He loves you."

Shrugging, Clarissa continued to swing. "Well, maybe he did," she said. "And Mary was pretty upset about it too. I'm sure she doesn't want to be stuck taking care of me."

"Did she say that?" Maggie asked.

Forcing herself to be honest, Maggie shook her head. "No, she didn't. She was nice to me and she was trying hard to be happy. But I could tell she was upset," she said. "And later on, I heard her talking to Mike. And Mike asked her if Bradley was abandoning Mary and me."

Pushing her feet against the sandy dirt, Clarissa started the swing moving higher into the sky.

"What did Mary say?" Maggie demanded, jumping off her swing.

Clarissa shrugged once again. "I don't know," she said. "I didn't want to hear any more, so I closed my door."

"Well, was he there when you got up this morning?" Maggie asked.

Shaking her head, Clarissa pumped her legs to bring the swing even higher, trying to hide her watery eyes from her friend. "No he wasn't," she said. "And I don't even care. If he wants to abandon me, I'll be fine. I did just fine by myself in Chicago and I can do fine in Freeport."

Maggie climbed back onto her swing, angrily pushing off the ground. "Of course you care," she said. "You can't lie to me, Clarissa. Did you ask Mike about it?"

"No," Clarissa replied angrily. "'Cause all he would do is lie to me."

"Angels can't lie," Maggie said. "So he would tell you the truth."

Clarissa continued to swing in silence while Maggie waited for her response. Finally, after a few minutes, Maggie sighed and just swung next to her friend in silence. They swung back and forth, the metal chains squeaking as they moved back and forth over the round casings that held them in place. The sun came out from behind a cloud and the girls could see their shadows gliding back and forth over the playground sand.

Finally Clarissa spoke. "Maggie."

"Uh, huh?"

"I didn't ask Mike because I was afraid he would say yes," she said softly.

"Isn't it better to know?" Maggie asked. "That way you can make plans."

A single tear slipped down Clarissa's cheek and she brushed it away quickly. "I guess," she said. "But he loved me before he and Mary got married. He always had time for me then."

Maggie stuck her legs straight out so her swing slowly lost altitude. "Maybe stuff changes when people get married. My parents aren't all goofy and lovey-dovey like Mary and Bradley."

"Maybe. And maybe if they weren't married any more he wouldn't want to abandon me," Clarissa said. "Maybe he's just tired of Mary."

Shrugging, Maggie hopped off the swing as the end-of-recess bell rang. "I don't think so, besides there's nothing you can do about that," she said.

Clarissa took her time sliding off the swing, a contemplative look on her face. "Well, maybe there is," she whispered to herself.

Chapter Twenty

Bradley hurried down the hall to the board room at the school district building. The walls filled with art from students throughout Freeport were incongruous with the thoughts racing through his mind. Each of the children recorded in the FBI reports had been students in the Freeport School District, even though they had been from not only the city of Freeport, but also the surrounding small towns. And except for Courtney Rasmussen, all of the children were also reported absent on the day of their disappearance. Although that could just point to a kidnapper who snatched children on their way to school, he had to wonder if it didn't have something to do with the school district itself.

The board room door was slightly ajar and Bradley entered without knocking. He had always felt that during an investigation he needed to place himself in a position of power and then watch the reaction of the people in the room. He noted, however, that the superintendent had the same idea about power, as the chair at the head of the table was filled by the superintendent and the one to his right, the subordinate seat, was left for Bradley.

Well, hell, Bradley thought, *good move, Nick, but I don't really need a seat.*

Striding to the front of the room and stopping in front of the large whiteboard, Bradley nodded to the eight people around the table. "Thank you all for being so prompt," he began. "Let's begin this meeting without delay."

Everyone but Nick Sears, the superintendent, had a good view of Bradley and the whiteboard, but Nick had to crane his neck in order to see.

"Nick, why don't you take the chair next to you, so you can get a better view of the whiteboard," Bradley suggested, biting back a smile.

Slightly disgruntled, Nick moved to the subordinate seat, sending Bradley a look of impatience. "Well, Alden, we don't have all day," he snapped. "Would you like to tell us why you've pulled us all together?"

"Julie, would you close the door?" Bradley asked.

Julie Quinn, the head of human resources, jumped up and closed the door.

"Thanks," Bradley said. "The information I share with you today is confidential, and normally I wouldn't be speaking with such a large group, but it is essential that we work together. As you know, another child was kidnapped yesterday. A child from the Freeport School District."

"Well, yes, but really, the school district has nothing to do with the kidnapping," Nick said, dismissing Bradley's comment.

"Actually, Nick, it does," Bradley said. "And I'll explain that correlation in a moment."

He paused, trying to decide how he was going to share information with the group without giving away too much. He suddenly realized that the kidnapper might be one of the people sitting in the meeting.

"But before I go any further, I'd like each of you to introduce yourselves and tell me how you interact with the attendance records for the district," he said. "Let's start with you, Nick."

"Actually, it's Dr. Sears," he began. "I have a Ph.D. in school administration."

What a jerk, Bradley thought.

"My apologies, Dr. Sears," Bradley said, emphasizing the word doctor. "Please continue."

"I actually have nothing to do with the attendance records," Nick said. "I leave those kinds of details to my subordinates."

"Well, actually," Julie Quinn, a middle-aged woman with graying hair, interjected, "you do see the attendance records, Dr. Sears. We put a report on your desk by ten o'clock every morning."

"Who else gets that report, Julie?" Bradley asked, cutting Nick off before he could argue.

Julie smiled at Bradley. "Well, actually, everyone at this table," she said. "Most of us get it as a hard copy, but Ray and Mark get it emailed to them."

"Ray?" Bradley asked, looking around the table.

An older man nodded and raised his hand; he had salt-and-pepper hair and an easy smile. "That's me, Ray Giles," he said. "I'm the truancy officer for the district. I get the reports every morning, although for the most part, I work off another report that lists the number of unexcused contiguous absences. I don't do much with that first report because the parents can call and excuse their child up to forty-eight hours after an absence."

"Who runs the other report?" Bradley asked.

"That would be me," a young man with shaggy hair raised his hand. "I'm Mark."

Mark was the only person in the room not dressed in business clothing. His Metallica t-shirt was faded and stretched out, and he looked like he had just rolled out of bed to attend the meeting.

"Mark," Bradley repeated. "What is your position?"

Shrugging, Mark leaned back in his chair and yawned. "Sorry," he apologized quickly. "I'm a computer consultant for the district. I work from my home office. Jules sends me the data and I run a bunch of reports, mostly for the state, you know, to get their funding. But I run other stuff too."

"Okay, thank you," Bradley said, turning to a young black woman dressed in a professional suit sitting next to Julie. "And what do you do?"

"I'm Angela Norris," she said, her voice clear and eloquent. "And I'm the Director of Equity. I collect, analyze and report data on equity programs and student performance."

"Do you receive the same reports as the others?" Bradley asked.

"I receive those reports and I also have Mark run reports for me that also focus on the students of color throughout the district," she said. "That would be the only report that would be different than the other people of the administrative team receive."

"Thank you, Angela," Bradley said.

"I'm Kelly, Kelly Sellers," said a young blonde woman wearing a low-cut blouse, seated across from Nick. "I'm Nick...I mean, the superintendent's secretary."

Bradley bit back a smile. *Yes, I bet you are.*

"Thank you, Kelly," Bradley said. "And are your reports any different from the others at the table?"

"How do you mean different?" she asked, confused.

He paused for a moment, trying to find the right words. "Other than the attendance report that Julie sends you, do you receive any other reports from Mark?"

She turned to Mark. "Do I receive any other reports from you?"

He shook his head. "No, sweetheart, just the attendance reports."

She smiled up at Bradley. "No, just the attendance reports."

"Thank you, Kelly," he said, trying to ignore the rolling eyes of most of the others at the meeting.

He did notice, however, that Nick didn't seem to be bothered by their responses. Of course, he also noted that Nick's eyes never traveled up further than Kelly's neckline.

There were two final people he hadn't met yet, one man and one woman. He started to turn to the woman, when the man interjected. "Excuse me, I don't mean to be rude," he said. "But I have to file my report with the state in thirty minutes. Do you think we are going to be much longer?"

"And you are?" Bradley asked.

"Ken Cannon," he replied, "I work in the Business Office. I'm a CPA."

"Ken, I will try to wrap this up quickly," he said. "Which reports do you receive?"

"Only attendance," he said. "And my report doesn't have any personal information in it. I just need the number of students absent and from which school. Then I can send the information to the state and run my numbers to make sure we are keeping close to budget."

"Budget?" Bradley asked.

"The state only pays us for the number of students per day," he said. "I try and estimate what our attendance will be and we build our budget on that. But, for example, if we get a bad case of flu and we have a lot of students missing school, I have to readjust the budget."

"Okay, thank you," he said, turning to the only person who hadn't introduced herself. "Hi, if you could…"

"I don't have to answer any of your questions," she blurted out. "My husband is a lawyer and he told me I didn't have to say anything to you."

"I'm sorry…" Bradley paused and waited.

"Kimberly…Kimberly Shelby," she replied.

He nodded and smiled at her. "Kimberly," he said. "I understand your apprehension, but this meeting is only informational. It might not lead to anything, but I need to dot all the i's and cross all the t's. Does that make sense?"

She nodded slowly. "So, you really are just looking into the disappearance of the little girl," she said, "not investigating any budgetary issues?"

Bradley saw Ken raise his eyebrow and look in Kimberly's direction. "Just the little girl," he said, wondering what in the world she was covering up.

"Okay, I get the reports every morning and I highlight them for any students under my area," she said. "Then, because my students are in special education classes, I make phone calls right away to be sure there isn't a problem."

"And that's all you do with the attendance report?" he asked.

Shrugging, she glanced around the room and bit her lower lip. "I also hand it out for scratch paper for some of the classes to use," she said.

"But that's confidential information," Julie exclaimed. "You should be shredding it."

"Well, I don't think that's very green," Kimberly argued. "Besides, I only let the younger classes use it, they can't even read."

"But their parents can, if they bring their work home," Bradley stated. "How soon, after a report is given to you, do you give the paper away?"

"I collect the reports from the week before and give it to them on Monday," she said. "So it's old by then."

Bradley took a deep breath. "Okay, one more question. Does anyone else share the reports with anyone else?"

Mark hesitantly raised his hand. "I've got a couple of interns who do work for me," he said. "Sometimes they look through the report. They know some of the kids from the school."

"How soon after you get the data do they see it?"

"Could be right away," he said. "We're networked together, so they know when it's in the file."

Julie shook her head. "Well, maybe we should just publish it in the paper."

"I don't think that's a good idea, Julie," Nick inserted pompously. "We really don't have the budget to do that."

"I was being facetious, Dr. Sears," she said.

"Oh, of course you were," he stammered. "Me too."

Most of these people are too stupid to be kidnappers, Bradley thought.

"Okay, thanks for your time," he said. "Julie, if I could ask you a couple of questions about the reports, I'd appreciate it."

"Sure Bradley," she replied. "Why don't you come down to my office?"

Bradley nodded to her, and then turned to Nick. "Thank you, Dr. Sears, for setting the time aside for your staff to meet with me," he said.

"Well, yes, of course," he blustered, getting out of his chair and walking over to Bradley. "We need to watch out for all of those little girls, don't we?"

Bradley looked down at the man who only reached halfway up his chest and nodded.

"Yes, we do," Bradley agreed. "Yes, we do."

Chapter Twenty-one

During the drive from the school district building back to City Hall, Bradley tried to put together all of the pieces of the puzzle. Julie had been able to track back and get attendance data on all of the missing children. Most of them had a long history of absences, so perhaps it had nothing to do with the reports. The superintendent rubbed him the wrong way, but that was mostly because the guy was a pompous ass. However, he did remember a Canadian study that suggested that short men were more likely to be sexual predators than their taller counterparts. He'd run a check on the doctor, as well as the programmer, the truancy officer and the accountant. With only girls missing, he had to believe they were looking for a man.

Looking down at the manila folder next to him, he was once again grateful for Julie. He knew she was bending the rules, but she copied the personnel records of all of the people in the meeting and sent it along with him. *Just in case you need it*, she had said when she handed it to him. He noticed she even included her own information. Shaking his head, he wondered how soon people would realize that she was the brains behind the school district and get rid of the pretender in the superintendent's office.

Pulling into his parking spot at City Hall, he noticed the Roadster parked across the street and groaned. "Crap, I forgot to call Mary this morning," he muttered.

Hurrying up the stairs, he stopped when he saw the door to the computer lab was open. Entering the room, he saw Mary and another woman working together at one of the older computer stations. He smiled proudly as he watched Mary focus entirely on what was in front of her. Whatever she was looking for, he knew she'd find it. He decided not to disturb their work and was stepping back when Mary turned and saw him.

"Oh, hello, Chief Alden," she said coolly. "I didn't see you. Of course, there's a lot of that happening lately."

She must be acting like she doesn't know me very well for the woman's sake, he thought.

"Mary," he said, with a smile. "I hope you're finding whatever you're looking for."

Mary's smile was slightly brittle. "I'm sure we will manage on our own," she replied. "I am really getting used to managing on my own."

Bradley cocked his head and met her eyes. *Yeah, this has nothing to do with anyone else. For some reason, Mary's upset. I wonder if something happened at the house.*

Entering the room, against his better judgment, he walked over to the two of them. "Hello, I'm Chief Alden," he said to the other woman.

100

Mary sighed. "I'm sorry, that was so rude of me," she apologized. "Celia, this is my husband, Bradley Alden."

Well, at least she's still acknowledging me as her husband.

"Bradley, this is Celia Rasmussen," Mary continued. "I'm working on a case with her."

"Rasmussen," Bradley mused. "Why does your name seem familiar?"

"My daughter, Courtney, was kidnapped eight years ago," she replied.

Bradley's heart dropped. *Of course,* he thought, *I was just reading the file this morning.*

"I'm so sorry about your daughter," he said. "I understand how it feels to have a loved one who's missing."

Celia looked up at his face and realized he did indeed seem to understand. "Thank you."

"Um, Mary, I was wondering if you had a moment or two?" he asked. "I wanted to speak with you privately."

Smiling politely, she shook her head. "Oh, sorry, I can't," she replied. "I'm sure you understand how work needs to take precedence over anything else. Perhaps you could email me."

He stared at her for a moment, trying hard to read her thoughts, but it was useless. "Yeah, of course, I'll send you an email," he said.

"Thanks," she said, turning back to the computer screen.

"Um, okay then," Bradley said, knowing he was just dismissed. "I'll just do that."

He backed out of the room and closed the door behind him.

As soon as she heard the click of the door, Mary exhaled sharply.

"So, you're pretty pissed off, huh?" Celia asked, biting back a smile.

"Was I that obvious?" she asked. "Sorry."

"So how long have you two been married?" she asked. "And what did he do?"

Mary chuckled. "Well, to answer your first question, we've been married nearly three weeks. And to answer your second question, he missed dinner last night, came home after I had gone to bed, fell asleep on the couch and then got up and left before we had a chance to speak this morning."

"Did it have anything to do with the missing girl?" Celia asked.

"What missing girl?"

"It was all over Facebook last night," Celia said. "A young girl, I think she was twelve years old, is missing. There's an Amber Alert out for her."

Mary felt like an idiot. "When was she reported missing?" she asked.

"Toward the end of the school day," Celia replied. "I understand they were searching for her until midnight, and then they started early this morning. I read the FBI came in early this morning to help with the search."

Mary pushed back her chair. "Would you excuse me for a few minutes? I've got to apologize to someone."

Nodding, Celia smiled. "Sure," she replied. "Take your time. I'll keep going through the files."

Chapter Twenty-two

The knock on his office door was tentative, unlike Dorothy's sharp and demanding one. "Come in," he called, looking up from the pile of paperwork before him.

Mary slipped just inside the office and closed the door. "Do you have a minute?" she asked quietly.

He stood, trying to read the new look on her face, and approached her tentatively. "Of course, but before you say anything, can I ask what you and Mrs. Rasmussen are working on?"

"Sure," she replied. "She hired me to help her find her daughter."

"Why?" he asked. "And I mean that in the nicest, most respectful way."

Mary smiled. "She read about me and she thinks she has seen her daughter," she said.

"Seen her? Where?"

"Bradley, seen her as a ghost," Mary explained. "On several occasions in her home."

He closed his eyes as anger and frustration bubbled up. "Damn it," he said. "I wonder how many more are dead."

"Well, we're not sure yet," Mary said. "I haven't confirmed she's dead. We're still researching information about the case."

"Would you be willing to share whatever you've found with me?" he asked. "I'm working on a similar case."

"Of course," she said eagerly. "I'll be happy to share it with you."

He paused to look down on her smiling face. "Um, whatever I did," he began. "I'm really sorry."

She sighed. "No, I'm sorry," she replied.

"Really?" he asked, brightening as he got closer. "For what?"

"For getting angry with you," she confessed.

He pulled her into his arms and just held her for a few moments. "This feels so good," he murmured into her hair. "I really missed you."

She wrapped her arms around him and laid her head against his chest. "I missed you too," she said.

He leaned away slightly and gently lifted her chin, lowering his lips to hers. At first the kiss was soothing and gentle, but Mary wanted more. She slid her hands from around his waist, up his chest and around his neck, burying her hands in his hair and pulling him closer.

He tightened his embrace, pulling her against him and crushing her mouth was his. The kiss lasted for a few delightful minutes until he pulled away. "Mary," he whispered hoarsely. "If we don't stop soon, Dorothy might be slightly embarrassed when she brings me the reports I requested."

She sighed and dropped her hands to his shoulders. "We couldn't just lock the door?" she asked.

He smiled broadly, enjoying the image playing out in his mind and then shook his head. "As much as I would really love to do that," he said. "We're going to have to save that fantasy for another time. And another place."

Grinning, she toyed with his top button. "Okay, but only if you promise to use the handcuffs," she teased.

He closed his eyes for a moment, trying to tamp down the rush of desire and shook his head. "You are going to be the death of me," he murmured, capturing her mouth with his one more time.

She responded to his kiss for a few moments of pure bliss and then stepped away. "You are going to be home tonight?" she asked breathlessly.

Eyes filled with passion, he nodded fervently. "Oh, yes," he breathed. "I'll be home tonight."

She took another step back, toward the door. "And even if you're late, you'll wake me up?"

He smiled widely. "Yes, I'll think of some way to wake you up."

"That sounds interesting, I might just go to bed early," she teased. "Just to see what you have in mind."

"I love you," he said, the teasing no longer in his eyes.

Love filled her heart to nearly bursting as she smiled back at him. "I love you too."

106

Chapter Twenty-three

Celia looked up as Mary entered the computer lab with a bright smile on her face. "So, the conversation went well?" she asked, biting back a smile.

Grinning, Mary nodded. "Really well," she said with a satisfied smile. "I think we got everything ironed out."

"Being a newlywed is hard work," Celia sympathized. "Especially when there are high-pressure jobs involved."

Sliding into her seat next to Celia, Mary nodded. "Yes, and add an eight-year-old daughter who was just reunited with her father to the mixture."

"Oh, wow," Celia said, nodding in agreement. "That does throw a little more interest into the pot."

"I like that, interest," Mary agreed. "But I'm sure everything will be great once we work out the kinks."

"That's the kind of attitude you need," Celia replied. "Don't let a couple bumps in the road get you down."

"So, what have you learned while I was gone?" Mary asked, turning her attention back to the computer screen.

Celia handed Mary her notepad. "I started with the names I had and looked up their cases, but quite a few of them had never been entered into the database. Then I did a search on missing children through the archived files and found four more who could fit our profile. If I add these new ones to the ones I already had...Mary, there have been at least a dozen missing children reports that seem to have similar attributes to Courtney's disappearance," she said.

"A dozen?" Mary repeated, shocked. "How could there be a dozen missing children and no one's connected them?"

Celia brought up the four files on the computer screen. "These were within Freeport and they were spaced several years apart," Celia explained. "But the ones in the articles were either from the rural areas, so the county sheriff handled those, or small towns with separate police districts."

Mary glanced through the reports. "All of them were young women, all of them were taken during the day, and none of their cases have been solved."

"I think most of them were considered to be runaways," Celia added, "because many of them had been troubled youth."

Mary sat back in her chair, reviewing the information in her mind. "I just spoke with Bradley about what we're working on," she said. "And he'd like us to share information with him. I told him we would; I hope you don't have a problem with that."

"No, if the newest missing girl is linked to Courtney's disappearance, maybe we can help her," Celia said.

"I'll see what he's learned and tell you about it tomorrow."

"So, what's the next step?" Celia asked, putting her files into her briefcase.

Mary glanced down at her watch; she had another hour before the school day was over.

"We have time for one more stop this afternoon."

"Where?" Celia asked.

Mary reached over and took hold of Celia's hands. "Let's go visit the park."

Chapter Twenty-four

Mary pulled the Roadster into a parking spot near the baseball diamonds and Celia pulled her red minivan into the next spot. The sun was beginning to lower in the western sky, but the day was still fairly mild and the ground was dry. The daffodils and crocuses in the superintendent's garden were in full bloom and the wind brought the scent of the spring flowers to both women.

"How are you doing?" Mary asked, walking over to Celia.

Taking a deep breath, Celia nodded. "I'm a little nervous I guess," she said. "I don't know if I'm ready to face reality."

Placing her hand on Celia's shoulder, Mary nodded. "We don't have to do this today," she said. "We don't ever have to do this."

"No. We do have to do this," Celia countered. "I have to do this. Not only for Courtney, but for myself."

"Okay," Mary agreed. "So, where was the picture taken?"

"Back behind the baseball field, toward the bridge that leads out of the park," Celia replied, pointing to a copse of trees just beyond the baseball field. "We can cut across here."

Mary walked slowly, taking in the scene around her and waiting for any indication that there were ghosts in the area. She started to follow Celia toward the trees when she felt a cold shiver down her spine. Turning, she saw a pretty teenage girl dressed in a softball uniform jogging toward the road. Her long hair was bouncing behind her as she ran.

The girl turned around, waved and then turned back toward the road, increasing her pace.

Mary hurried after her, staying on the road to avoid any new obstacles, but always keeping the girl within eyesight. As she entered the bridge the girl stopped and seemed to be talking with someone. She shook her head with a smile on her face and then shrugged and walked over to the other side of the bridge. A moment later she was gone.

Mary hurried to the bridge, looking around for any other trace of the girl. "Courtney?" she called. "Courtney, can you hear me?"

Suddenly, a movement in the distance caught her eye. The image was blurry, like Mary was looking through pouring rain into a window, but she could see it was Courtney. The girl's terror-filled eyes met hers as she watched the image move further and further away.

"Mary?"

Mary jumped and gasped, and then turned to see Celia standing next to her. "Oh, you scared me to death," she said.

"I heard you yelling," Celia said. "So I rushed over. What happened?"

Mary took a deep breath. "I saw Courtney," she said. "I watched her as she waved goodbye to her friends and jogged across the park in the rain."

Inhaling sharply, Celia nodded. "What happened?"

"She jogged down the road and stopped at the bridge," Mary continued, replaying the scene in her mind. "She was on the pavement, but she stepped up on the curb."

"There must have been a car coming," Celia explained. "The bridge is too narrow for a person and a car."

Nodding, Mary walked closer to the bridge. "She stopped and spoke with someone," she said. "It must have been the person in the car. She smiled at him and shook her head. Then she shrugged, walked around the other side of the bridge and disappeared."

"She got into a car?" Celia asked.

"Yes, but she knew the person," Mary said. "She talked with them and even laughed with them. She initially turned the ride down, but for some reason decided to get in."

"Did you see anything else?" Celia asked.

"Yes. I did," Mary said, nodding slowly. "I saw her image, like she was in a car in the pouring rain, going up the road until they disappeared."

Celia leaned against the side of the bridge and started to weep. She slipped down to the ground and laid her head on her knees as the pain tore through her. "She's dead," she cried. "My baby's dead."

Mary knelt down and put her arms around the sobbing woman. She just let her cry for a few minutes, releasing some of the grief she was experiencing. "I'm so sorry, Celia," she finally whispered hoarsely. "I'm so very sorry."

"No. Don't be sorry," Celia said, her voice catching. "At least...at least I know."

Helping Celia to her feet, Mary placed her arm around the woman's waist and they walked back to their cars in silence, Celia softly crying into her tissue. When they reached the cars, Mary stopped next to the red minivan. "Do you want me to come home with you?" she asked.

Wiping her eyes, Celia took a deep breath. "No, but thank you," she said. "I need to be alone for a while. I'll meet you at your office tomorrow morning. Okay?"

Mary hugged her once more. "Sure. But if you need to talk, don't hesitate to call me," she insisted.

"Thank you, Mary," she said, as she unlocked her car. "I'll remember that."

Watching the minivan drive off, Mary ached for her new friend. But she understood, better than most, the best thing she could do for Celia was to find the person who had killed her daughter.

Chapter Twenty-five

"Chief Alden," Bradley's voice boomed in her cell phone.

"Hi," she replied. "Do you have a minute?"

"Sure, what's up?" he asked.

"Courtney Rasmussen is dead," she replied, her eyes filling with tears. She took a deep breath and continued. "I saw her ghost in the park."

"Damn it," Bradley said softly. "Does her mother know?"

Nodding, even though he couldn't see her, Mary replied, "Yes, she was here in the park with me."

"How's she doing?"

"Well, you know," she said, her voice breaking. "It's pretty much the worst day of your life when you find out your loved one is dead."

She wiped the tears away with a swipe of her arm and took another deep breath. "She's upset. She's crying and she says she needs to be alone."

"And how are you taking it?" Bradley asked gently.

"I hate it," Mary replied, tears flowing steadily now. "I hate telling people things that change their lives for the worse. I hate making people cry. I hated making Celia cry."

"Do you want me to be logical or just understanding?" he asked.

A soft gurgle of laughter escaped her lips and she sniffed back some tears. "Understanding at first, then logical," she replied, pulling a handful of tissues out of the box on the seat of her car and blotting her eyes and nose.

"Okay, you've got it," he said, a touch of sadness in his voice. "It's not fair that you have to tell people about their loved ones. It's not fair that you are given situations where you can't fix anything; you just have to stand by and watch bad things happen. It's not fair that you are so tenderhearted that every ghost you meet and every person you help steals away a bit of your heart."

Sniffing again, she nodded. "That was very good," she replied.

Chuckling softly, he continued. "But…"

"Are you doing logical already?" she complained.

"Yes," he said, "because you need the logic now. Let me ask you, do we know more about Courtney's death than we ever did before?"

"Yes," she agreed.

"And now are we closer to catching the person who did it?"

"I think so."

"And that's true for all the people you have helped. You didn't cause the situation. But you are a solution for people who are hopeless. You don't cause the pain, Mary, you offer hope."

115

"But it still hurts," she said softly.

"Of course it does," he replied, "because you care about people. And that's one of the reasons I love you."

"I love you too," she responded, wiping her eyes once again.

"Yeah, I know," he said. "And that makes me the luckiest guy in the world."

She took a deep breath and nodded through her tears. "Thank you for talking to me," she said. "It really helped."

"Good," he said. "So, I can be home around eight-thirty. Will that work?"

She thought for a moment. "Well, I'll give Clarissa her dinner early, but let her stay up a little late, so when you get home, she can spend some time with you," Mary suggested. "Then, I'll have our dinner ready at about nine-fifteen or so. How does that sound?"

"It sounds perfect," he replied. "Thank you for being so understanding."

She felt a twinge of guilt at being less than understanding these past few days, but brushed it off. "No problem," she said. "I'll see you at eight-thirty."

Chapter Twenty-six

"Clarissa," Mary called from the kitchen. "Dinner will be ready in a few minutes, so wash up and come downstairs."

A few minutes later Clarissa jogged down the stairs, stopping several steps before the floor. "Isn't my dad home?" she asked.

Wiping her hands on a kitchen towel, Mary walked over to the entrance of the living room. "No, honey, remember I told you he had to work late," she explained. "So, I'm going to have you eat your dinner early so you have time to visit with him later."

Folding her arms over her chest, Clarissa glared at Mary. "I don't want to eat early," she said. "I want to eat with my father."

"Well, sorry, that's just not going to work tonight," Mary replied, heading back into the kitchen. "But maybe later this week he can be home on time and you can eat with him."

Pulling the bubbling casserole of homemade macaroni and cheese out of the oven, Mary placed it on a trivet on the counter. She pulled a plate down from the cabinet and added some of the pasta, a green salad and some sliced chicken breast. "I made you all of your favorites," she continued, "to make up for not eating with him."

"I hate all of that," Clarissa replied, as she walked to the kitchen doorway and slumped against the frame.

Mary picked up the plate and brought it over to the table, placing it in front of Clarissa's chair. "Wow, that's too bad," Mary said. "Because that's what's on the menu tonight."

"I bet you aren't going to eat this kind of food when my dad gets home," she argued. "I bet you're going to have some really good stuff."

Mary walked back to the counter, stuck a fork into the macaroni and cheese and took a bite. "This is really good stuff," she said, enjoying the thick cheesy sauce and soft noodles so much she took another fork-full. "Actually, this is pretty much incredible."

"Well, I'm not going to eat it," Clarissa shouted.

Mary nodded, sticking the fork back into the pan. "Okay, I'll call you when Bradley gets home."

"What?" the child asked, astonished.

"I'll call you when your dad gets home," Mary repeated. "You can just do your homework for now."

"But I'm starving," Clarissa said.

Mary looked up at her and smiled. "Oh, well, good," she said. "Your dinner is on the table."

"But I want something else," she insisted.

Shaking her head, Mary scooped up one more fork-full. "There isn't anything else for dinner," she said. "This is it."

Mary watched the internal struggle the child was having and, although she didn't understand why Clarissa was being so disagreeable, made sure she kept her face as neutral as possible.

"Fine," Clarissa finally exclaimed. "I'll eat it."

She stormed from the doorway to the table and shoved her chair a few inches back in order to sit in it. Then she proceeded to shove the food into her mouth without attempting any conversation with Mary.

Picking up a glass of ice water, Mary walked over to the table and sat across from her daughter. "So, how was school today?" she asked politely, sipping slowly on the water.

Clarissa looked down at her plate and continued to eat, ignoring Mary.

"It's about time we did some shopping for spring and summer clothes, don't you think?" Mary asked. "I think you could probably use some new shoes too."

Shoving an oversized helping of macaroni and cheese into her mouth, Clarissa nearly choked rather than answer the question.

Mary took another sip of water and acted as if she didn't realize Clarissa was being rude. "I'm so glad you changed your mind about the dinner," she said brightly. "It seems as though you were starving. Would you like a little more?"

Clarissa set down her fork, glared at Mary across the table and then darted from the room and up the stairs. Sighing, Mary collected up the empty plate and utensils and took them over to the sink.

"I would have gotten my bottom spanked for that kind of behavior," Mike said, appearing next to the counter. He looked down at the casserole and smiled. "Now that looks, excuse the pun, heavenly."

"Thanks," Mary replied, stepping over and taking one more taste. "It really tastes good too. And I don't seem to be able to resist it."

"So, why didn't you?" he asked.

"Why didn't I what? Tan her hide?" Mary replied with a smile.

"Yeah, or stand her in the corner, or give her a time out, or whatever it is parents do these days."

Giving up, Mary pulled a bowl from the cabinet, filled it with the macaroni and cheese and brought it over to the table. She sat down and took a bite before replying. "Today I sat with a woman who learned that her daughter had been killed eight years ago," Mary said. "She had a feeling it had happened, but today I had the distinct privilege of confirming that for her, killing any hope she might have had lingering in her heart."

Mike leaned over and placed his hand over hers. "Mary, I'm sorry."

She shrugged, wiping a stray tear away. "Well, anyway, I guess Clarissa's temper tantrum didn't seem to be that big of a deal, considering," she said. "And it must be tough for her to adjust, once again, to our new household."

She took another bite and then smiled. "Besides, I'm the stepmother," she said. "I think it's my duty to be exceptionally nice and remove the stigma that has been perpetuated by storytellers for generations."

Smiling, Mike nodded. "I'm sure stepmothers all over the world are thanking you for your patience. But have you considered what lesson she learned tonight?"

Mary took another bite and contemplated his comment. Finally, she spoke, "Well, let's see…she was rude and demanding and didn't want to eat what I had made for her. I was polite and firm and didn't let her bully me or make me angry. She ended up eating what I had cooked and I didn't let her bother me. I think she learned that polite and firm wins."

Mike wasn't convinced. "I don't know, Mary," he said. "Something tells me she has not even begun to fight."

"Mike, don't worry," Mary said. "I'm sure everything will be fine."

Chapter Twenty-seven

Driving slowly through the streets of Freeport, he checked his review mirror a number of times. So far no one seemed to be following him, but he had been spooked by the meeting with the Chief of Police all day. *Did he know something more than he let on,* he wondered. *Was he just waiting for someone to show fear?*

He pulled to a stop at an intersection, waiting for the light to turn green, and thought about the little girl waiting for him in his basement, and for a moment, the worries of the day disappeared. He slowly moistened his lips with his tongue, anticipating how she would taste. His hands gripped the steering wheel tighter as he envisioned her young, slender form. He smiled when he thought about the stark fear burning in her eyes as he taught her the lessons of the day.

He had always wanted to be a teacher, he thought, his mood turning melancholy. He had always wanted to be near children. Small children. Little girls.

The harsh beep of a car's horn startled him. He looked around, surprised that cars were moving around him and the light had been green for a while. He smiled into his rearview mirror, waved at the car behind him in apology as he accelerated and moved through the intersection. *Insolent idiot*, he silently fumed at the driver, *go around me next time. I'm sure you don't have anything to do that's as important as what I have to do.*

Turning right onto the residential road, he entered the tree-covered lane and felt some of the anxiety lessen. The houses that bordered the meandering street were set far apart from each other and backed up to the edge of Krape Park. It was like entering a hidden valley, where you could find solitude, rest and privacy. His smile widened. *Privacy. Yes, that is very important to me and all of the students who have enjoyed the pleasure of my tutelage.*

A discreet tap on the remote had the large gates to his driveway opening for him. He drove through, smiling wryly at the words on the bronze plaque inserted into the stone post on the left side. *Pine Haven.* He pressed the remote again and the gates closed and locked.

The evening was clear and calm, so he rolled down his window and enjoyed the pungent smell from all of the young pine trees that had been planted during the past ten years in his large yard. "Hello girls," he whispered. "Soon another young sapling will join your ranks."

Chapter Twenty-eight

"Daddy, I'm so glad you're home!" Clarissa cried, leaping off the bottom step and throwing herself into his arms as he walked through the door.

"Clarissa, sweetheart, what's wrong?" Bradley asked, kneeling down and embracing the sobbing child.

"I'm so glad you're here," she wept. "I was so afraid."

Holding her shoulders, he gently pushed her back a little to look at her face. "Why are you afraid?"

"Because Mary hates me," she whimpered. "She doesn't want me to be here. She told Mike that you were going to abandon me."

Bradley looked up to see surprise on Mary's face as she hurried into the living room. "Clarissa, I don't hate you," she said, kneeling down next to the child. "And I'm very sorry that you misunderstood me. But your father and I are not going to abandon you."

She laid her hand on Clarissa's shoulder, only to have it shrugged off as Clarissa clung to her father. "She's lying," she cried. "She made me eat dinner tonight all by myself and even when I told her my stomach hurt, she still made me eat it. I had to go upstairs and throw up."

"What?" Mary asked. "You didn't tell me you were sick."

Burying her head deeper into her father's shoulder, she continued to cry. "I tried to tell her, but she was too busy laughing with Mike," she said. "She never, ever listens to me. She just sends me up to my room as soon as I get home from school."

Bradley met Mary's eyes over his daughter's head and saw that she was deeply troubled by Clarissa's accusations. He also knew that Mary would never do anything to cause harm or discomfort to the child. But something was up with Clarissa and he didn't think he would be able to find out while she was in Mary's presence. He winked at Mary and sent her what he hoped was a reassuring smile, picked Clarissa up in his arms and carried her toward the stairs. "Come on, sweetheart," he said. "Let's have a little talk."

Her heart sinking, Mary watched Bradley and Clarissa go upstairs. She really wanted to follow, wanted to be part of the conversation to find out what in the world was happening with Clarissa. But she knew it wouldn't be helpful, so she sat down on the couch and waited.

"No one told me kids could be so difficult," Mike said, appearing next to her on the couch.

"Yeah, tell me about it," Mary replied. "From her description, you'd think I was the evil stepmother."

"Yeah, I know," he said. "I can't believe you were going to abandon her."

125

Mary turned quickly to face him. "Mike," she said sharply.

Grinning, he shook his head. "I was joking," he replied. "We all know she was being overly dramatic. We also all know you, and know you would die before either hurting Clarissa or letting someone else hurt her. So stop worrying and let Bradley handle it."

"I suppose you're right."

"Babe, I'm always right," he said. "See, that's where you made your mistake. I was Mr. Right and you didn't see it."

A shadow of a smile flitted across her face. "Mike, you were already dead."

"Babe, then I was dead-right."

Shaking her head and chuckling, she stood up and walked toward the kitchen. "Well, I guess I should put some of the dinner things away until Bradley gets downstairs," she said. "I don't want his dinner to be ruined."

"Hey, he'll be down in a few minutes," he said. "I heard Clarissa asking him to read her a story."

"She'll probably ask for the entire *Encyclopedia Britannica*," Mary muttered.

Shaking his head, Mike floated over. "No, I think she asked for the Old Testament," he teased. "But at least it has a good message."

Groaning, Mary shook her head. "You are really not helping," she said.

"Hey, don't worry about it, kid," he said softly and then he grinned. "This too shall pass."

"Go away," she chuckled.

He started to fade. "Your wish is my command," he teased. "I'll go upstairs and keep an eye on things."

Mary filled the dishwasher, cleaned the counters and did anything else she could to keep herself busy in the kitchen while she waited for Bradley to come downstairs. Finally, after waiting for an hour, she opened the freezer, pulled out a pint of dark chocolate ice cream, opened a drawer and pulled out a spoon. "I'll just have a couple of spoonfuls," she promised herself as she headed to her recliner to watch the news.

Thirty minutes later, the news program ended and Mary looked down in dismay at the empty container of ice cream in her hand. "Well, so much for self-control," she said. "I'll just have a salad for dinner whenever Bradley comes down."

Bringing the container and spoon back into the kitchen, she was slightly alarmed when she saw that it was already past ten o'clock. "If he stays up there much longer, I'll be making him breakfast."

Hurrying up the stairs, she walked softly down the hallway, trying to make as little noise as possible. Standing outside Clarissa's bedroom door, she grasped the door handle and waited, listening for any sounds coming from the room. Finally, she slowly turned the knob and pushed the door open slightly. Through the light from the bedside lamp, she could see that Clarissa was sound asleep in her bed and Bradley was sleeping in the rocking chair next to her. Smiling wryly, she tiptoed into the room and bent close to Bradley's ear. "Bradley," she whispered. "You need to go to bed."

"Mmmmmm?" he whispered back, his eyes not opening.

She gently jiggled his shoulder. "You need to go to bed," she repeated softly. "Or you will have a terrible backache in the morning."

Opening his eyes, he looked up at her and smiled. "Hi," he said. Then everything seemed to click into place as he looked around the room and saw Clarissa asleep in her bed. He turned back to Mary and shook his head. "Oh, Mary, I'm so sorry."

She kissed him on the cheek and smiled. "No problem," she said. "I know you were exhausted. Do you want something to eat or do you just want to sleep?"

He stood, nearly stumbling, and she led him out of the room, closing the door softly behind them. He yawned widely and leaned against the wall. "I think I'm more tired than hungry," he said. "Do you mind?"

"No, actually, I find that I'm not very hungry either," she replied. "Let's just go to bed."

Chapter Twenty-nine

Mary grabbed another Diet Pepsi from the little refrigerator in her office and glanced at the clock; it was only nine-thirty. *It's going to be a very long day.*

Sitting back down at her desk, she opened the file Celia had left for her and started reading through all of the case files. "Hey, you got another one of those?" a female voice asked.

Mary looked up and was surprised to see Tracey Bresnahan, the writer turned spy, standing inside her office. "How did you...?" Mary began, looking up at the small bell over her front door.

"Trick of the trade," Tracey interrupted with a smile. "So, how's married life?"

Getting up and pulling another soda out of the refrigerator, Mary gave herself a moment to school her thoughts. It wouldn't do to give too much of their private life away to Tracey and the organization she worked with. "Married life is great," Mary finally replied, handing Tracey the drink. "Although I have to admit, it's tough getting back to reality once you've been on an extended honeymoon."

Sitting down in the chair on the other side of the desk, Tracey leaned back, took a sip of the Diet Pepsi and sighed. "I remember my honeymoon," she said. "We went camping. It was not nearly as romantic or comfortable as a castle in Scotland."

So, we are going to chit chat for a while, Mary thought. *Okay, I can play that game.*

"It was wonderful," Mary said. "I could get used to living in the lap of luxury."

Tracey placed the can on a coaster on the desk and met Mary's eyes. "I understand that someone from the agency met with you when you were there," she said.

So much for chit chat.

"Yes, we went into town and met him at a local pub," Mary said. "It was quite an interesting meeting."

Chuckling, Tracey nodded. "More interesting for him because of all the notoriety you two had garnered."

Shrugging, Mary bit back a smile. "Well, I had no idea that Headless Hannah had been such a celebrity in the area. She was a lovely woman, once you got to know her, and deserved her rest."

"Yes, and the staff and most of the countryside considered you a hero for helping her get that rest," Tracey replied.

"Well," Mary did allow herself to smile, "I suppose it would be a little disconcerting to have a woman walk into your bedroom at night carrying her head on a platter."

Shaking her head, Tracey picked up her soda once again; she lifted it as a toast in Mary's direction. "Well, here's to you for not only getting rid of a

130

celebrated ghost, but for knocking the socks off the London office."

"I knocked their socks off?" she replied, pleased with herself.

"Yes, and that's why I'm here," Tracey said.

Send me back to Scotland, Mary pleaded silently, *until Clarissa is sixteen years old.*

"Something wrong?" Tracey asked, cocking her head slightly, trying to read Mary's face.

"No, I'm just adjusting to having a husband, an eight-year-old daughter and a business," she answered. "It's a little challenging."

"I should say so," Tracey agreed, "which is why I think you'll be pleased with the agency's decision."

"And that is?"

"The agency wants you and Bradley to maintain your covers," she said, "especially while you are raising children. You aren't going to be field agents yet, only consultants, but they can call you into service under certain extenuating circumstances."

"And that means?" Mary asked.

Tracey smiled. "That means you're stuck in Freeport at least until Clarissa is an older teen and capable of taking care of herself."

"Wait," Mary said. "Not that I'm not appreciative of their sensibilities, but I don't get this."

"The agency is interested in you and Bradley as a unique husband and wife team," she said. "They have noted how well you work together. They have also found, however, when there are small children at home, agents in the field make mistakes because they are worried about what's going on at home, rather than the objective. They would rather use you both, as the need warrants, as consultants, then wait for a few years and use you both as field agents."

"So, when Clarissa is a teenager, they will start using us as field operatives?" Mary asked.

Tracey nodded. "Well, unless you have additional children and then they would wait until the youngest is old enough to be independent."

"The likelihood of me getting pregnant is somewhere between slim and none," Mary said.

"Okay then, you'll be qualified for field work in eight years or so," Tracey said. "But I have a feeling we'll be using you for consulting much sooner than that."

Standing, Tracey leaned over the table and extended her hand. Mary stood and shook Tracey's hand. "Thanks for stopping by," Mary said.

"I'm really looking forward to working with you," Tracey said. "I'll be in touch."

Once Tracey had left her office, Mary sat back in her chair and closed her eyes. She could really use a nap. She had tossed and turned all night, concerned about Clarissa's behavior, and when she had finally fallen asleep she found herself dreaming the same dream from the night before, searching for the lost child.

"I am just losing it," she murmured.

Smiling briefly, she remembered waking up and curling into Bradley's embrace. He had held her as she told him about the dream and then he kissed her in a way that woke up every single cell in her body. They had just begun making up for their missed opportunities the night before when Clarissa yelled for him.

Mary sighed and took another sip of soda. *She is an eight-year-old child,* she told herself. *She is not doing this on purpose. She is a little confused and is just trying to figure things out. That's all.*

Chapter Thirty

"It was so great last night," Clarissa laughed as she pushed herself higher on the swing. "I told Bradley that Mary hated me and she made me eat food so I would be sick."

"What did she make you eat?" Maggie asked, swinging next to her.

"Macaroni and cheese," Clarissa replied.

"But that's your favorite, why did it make you sick?"

"It didn't really make me sick," she said, rolling her eyes. "I just told him that, so he would hate her."

"But he loves her," Maggie said.

She shook her head. "No, he doesn't," she argued, her stomach tightening as she argued. "He just wanted a mother for me, so he married her. Just like in Cinderella."

Maggie stopped her swing and turned to Clarissa. "No, he wanted to marry her even before he knew about you."

"Well, now he loves me better," she said angrily. "And since I'm just a little girl and she's a grown up, he needs to take care of me, not her."

"Why can't he take care of both of you?"

Clarissa stopped her swung, jumped out of it and faced her friend. "Don't you get it?" she asked.

"If they get divorced, then Bradley will need me. He won't have any other children. He won't have a wife. It will just be me and my dad."

"That's never going to work," Maggie said.

"Sure it will," Clarissa argued. "Last night I made him stay in my room and read to me until he fell asleep in the chair. He left Mary sitting downstairs waiting for him. She was going to make a special dinner and everything and instead, he was with me."

"So, that's only one time."

"And then, this morning, I waited outside their door until I heard them talking," she said. "Then I went back to my room and screamed for him, like I was having a bad dream. He came running in right away and I made him stay with me until it was time to get ready to go to school."

"That was mean," Maggie said. "Mary's not being mean to you, but you're being mean to her."

Clarissa folded her arms across her chest and shook her head. "I'm not being mean," she said. "I'm working out a plan. My plan."

Maggie slipped from the swing and walked over to her friend. "I think it's a bad plan. I think it's a mean plan. Mary helped find you – Mary helped your mother. The bad man would have you if Mary hadn't done everything she did," Maggie yelled.

"I don't believe you," Clarissa said.

"You know I'm right," Maggie insisted. "You know Mary is trying hard to be a good mother."

Clarissa pressed her lips close together and shook her head. "You don't understand," she finally said.

"Understand what?"

"If Mary and Bradley stay married, then they have each other," she explained. "They don't need me."

"'Course they don't need you," Maggie said. "They want you."

"No," Clarissa replied, tears filling her eyes. "Maybe your family wants you. But only my 'doptive parents wanted me. I'm just an obligation."

"No, Clarissa, you have it all wrong," Maggie said. "Mary and Bradley want you."

"Until they have kids of their own," she argued. "Then they won't need me anymore. So, I'm not going to let that happen."

She started to turn, but Maggie stopped her by putting a hand on her shoulder. "I can't help you hurt Mary. She's my friend."

"That's fine," Clarissa snapped back. "I'll just do it on my own."

Chapter Thirty-one

A light tap on her office door had Mary glancing up from her computer screen and looking over to see Celia entering the room. "Hi," Mary said with a hesitant smile. "How are you doing?"

Celia sat down across from Mary and took a deep breath. "I had a pretty bad night," she confessed. "But I finally realized that it was far better to know than it was to only guess."

Mary sat back and looked at her new friend. Her face was still pale and there were dark shadows beneath her eyes. Although she was bravely trying to smile, Mary could see the tremor on her lips and the tight grasp she had on the handle of her briefcase. She was definitely a woman close to the edge.

"You know, you don't have to be brave," Mary finally said. "There is nothing wrong with showing your emotions. As a matter of fact, it's healthier to let them out."

Shaking her head, Celia gripped her briefcase tighter. "I'm afraid," she said softly. "I'm afraid that if I start to cry, I will never be able to stop."

"I really do understand that feeling," Mary said, as an idea came to her.

Glancing at her watch, she stood up and smiled at Celia. "Bradley and I didn't have a chance to talk about the case last night, so we have a meeting scheduled here in about an hour. But in the meantime, I have an idea that might help you feel better. Let's go visit an old friend of mine."

After locking up the office, Mary guided Celia down the street and around the block to an old abandoned building on Spring Street. The building was a large brownstone with a heavy front door made of glass.

"Where are we?" Celia asked. "It looks like it's closed down."

Mary smiled. "Well, normally it is," she said. "But I have a feeling that my good friend Ernie will open up for us."

She walked to the entrance, wiping away the dirt on the window.

Celia followed close behind her and peered over her shoulder to read the faded white letters on the door: *Ernie's Gymnasium and Pugilism Training.*

"Can I just ask what we're doing?"

Mary looked over her shoulder to Celia. "We're going the distance."

Turning back to the door, Mary knocked lightly. "Hey Ernie, I have a friend who could use a round or two," she said.

"Really, Mary, I don't think we should be drinking this early in the morning," Celia inserted.

Mary listened for the lock on the other side to click and pushed the door open before she looked over her shoulder. "The only thing we'll be drinking in here is water," she said, entering the dark building.

Celia followed closely behind her. "I'm beginning to agree with some of those not-so-nice comments about you on the Internet," she said quietly, as she peered into the darkness.

"No, you don't," Mary replied confidently. "Because if you really thought I was nuts, you'd be really nice to me. And that last comment was nearly rude."

In spite of herself, Celia smiled as she held on to the back of Mary's coat.

Reaching inside her pocket, Mary pulled out a small flashlight. The scent of dried wood, aging leather and dust was as strong as it had been the first time she's been there. Dust motes floated all around her, highlighted in the beams of morning light that slipped through the planking on the tall side windows. But this time, she knew where she was going. Walking over to a large gray box in another corner of the room, Mary wiped the spider webs off the front and pulled the metal switch down. The fluorescent bulbs in the hanging ceiling fixtures slowly fluttered to life. They started at the far end of the room and slowly each area of the gym was filled with light.

"Hey, sister, how've you been?" Ernie asked, appearing in the middle of the boxing ring situated in the center of the room. "And who's the doll you've got with you?"

Mary grinned as the ghost materialized before her. She hadn't seen him since Linda's wedding, but she had hoped he was still around. His graying hair

139

was still styled in a crew cut and the face below was wide, with a strong and stubborn jaw. His nose looked like it had been broken a number of times and his broad grin advertised the wide gap between his upper teeth. She winked slyly at him, not letting Celia know there was someone else in the room with them.

"Celia, my friend Ernie owns this place," Mary explained. "He helped me through the tough times by training me. I thought it might do you some good to punch something, really hard."

"You ain't gonna tell her I'm here," Ernie teased. "Are you?"

"Not yet," Mary whispered.

"What did you say?" Celia asked.

"I said, not yet," she repeated. "You can't punch anything until you put the gloves on."

She led Celia to a corner of the room where a large, brown, leather punching bag hung from a beam. Next to it, a series of smaller bags were suspended at head level. The leather was old and worn, but the bag was still intact. Celia ran a hand over it. "Will it hold up to a good punch?" she asked.

Ernie laughed. "Tell her to give it all she's got."

Mary picked up a pair of old boxing gloves and handed them to Celia. "Give it all you've got," she repeated.

Slipping the gloves on, Celia hesitantly punched the bag.

"She throws a punch like a girl," Ernie complained. "Show her how to do it right."

Mary picked up a pair of gloves for herself and stood next to Celia. "Okay, let me show you the right way to throw a punch," she said. "And then I'm going to stand back and let you give it hell."

Nearly an hour later, the bag still gently swaying in the air, Celia stepped back, pushed her hair back in place with her gloved hands and turned back to Mary. "I do feel much better," she panted.

"She's got some potential," Ernie added, walking around her slowly. "She's got looks and she's tough. She ought to consider roller-derby."

Biting back a snort, Mary helped Celia unlace her gloves. "Just let me know if you want to come back," she said. "I have a feeling Ernie wouldn't mind in the least."

Chapter Thirty-two

Mary and Celia arrived back at the office just as Bradley was pulling his cruiser into the parking spot out front next to the Roadster. "Field trip?" he asked, as he met them at the door.

"I introduced Celia to Ernie's place," Mary explained. "It was...therapeutic."

Raising an eyebrow, Bradley leaned over and whispered into Mary's ear. "Did she meet Ernie?"

Laughing, Mary shook her head. "No," she said in a normal voice. "Ernie and Celia didn't get the chance to meet."

"No, although, from what Mary told me about him, he seems like a very nice man," Celia said. "I'd like to meet him someday."

"He's a great guy," Bradley agreed. "And he taught Mary a couple things about throwing a punch."

"That's what she said," Celia said. "Although I don't understand what she meant about being the hit of a wedding."

Chuckling, Bradley smiled down at his wife. "Someday, when you've gotten to know each other a little better, I'm sure she'll tell you the whole story," he explained.

"Yes," Mary agreed, "later, when you won't think I'm crazy."

Smiling sadly, Celia placed her hand on Mary's arm. "After our experience yesterday afternoon, I promise, I won't ever think you're crazy."

"Thank you," Mary said. "I really appreciate that."

Nodding, Celia stepped back. "Well, I'm going to get out of your way so you can meet," she said. "If you need anything, please call me."

"I will," Mary said. "Thanks again."

Bradley opened the door for Mary and they both entered the office.

"She's a very nice lady," Bradley said.

"Yes, she is," Mary agreed. "And I'm sure she was a wonderful mother. It's not fair."

Following her over to her desk, he sat down across from her. "You're right, it's not," he agreed. "And all we can do at this point is try and bring her some closure."

Bradley watched the determination form on Mary's face as she pulled her notepad across her desk. "You're absolutely right," she said. "So, what do you have?"

After sharing the highlights of the meeting, Bradley gave her copies of all the reports he had. "So, now you know what I know," he said.

"No one stands out?" she asked. "No gut feelings?"

"Well, the superintendent is a jerk," he said. "But that doesn't make him a murderer."

143

"It doesn't make him not a murderer either," Mary added.

"So, what did you learn from Courtney?" he asked.

Sitting back in her chair, she paused for a moment, gathering her thoughts. "I saw her walking away from the softball diamond, waving at friends," she said.

"So it happened right after practice, when there were still people in the park," Bradley said.

Mary nodded. "Her hair and face began to show signs of rain," she explained, "and then she started jogging down the road toward the bridge that leads to Demeter Avenue."

"She lived off of Demeter," he said. "So she was on her way home."

"She was on the bridge and then stepped up to the curb," Mary said.

"A car was coming," he surmised.

"Yes, I think that's what happened," she agreed. "Then she stopped walking and spoke with someone. At first she shook her head and then she laughed. She stepped off the curb, walked to the other side of the bridge and disappeared."

"She got into a car with someone," he said. "Someone she knew."

"Yes, her actions didn't show any fear or reservation," she said. "He probably offered her a ride home in the rain."

Bradley pulled Courtney's police report out of the file. "Her parents reported her missing at about seven o'clock that night," he said. "Softball practice ended at five and the storm began at about five-fifteen."

"So, there was nearly two hours of time for the perp to take her somewhere," Mary said.

"That's what the initial theory was," Bradley said. "Someone from out of town had taken her and by the time she was reported, they could have been in Chicago. No one saw anything."

"Well, everyone was hurrying home to get out of the rain," Mary said. "It was a perfect opportunity."

Nodding, Bradley stared at the report again. "So, if we presume that Courtney is another victim of the same person who kidnapped the rest of the girls," he said slowly. "We need to not only determine the points that are the same about all these crimes, but also what's different."

Opening her own file, she nodded and jotted down some notes. "Okay, same, she is a young girl that attends Freeport schools."

"Different – she did not have a history of skipping school," Bradley said.

"Different – it didn't happen during the school day," she added.

Bradley stopped scanning the report and looked up at Mary. "Okay, that's a big different," he said. "Because if our perp had a system of trolling the streets looking for kids who had skipped school, why would he be at the park at the end of the day?"

"You're right," Mary agreed, eagerly shaking her head. "The park has too many people and too many adults for him to feel as safe as he felt driving down empty residential streets during the school day."

"So, if he wasn't going through the park to find his next victim..." Bradley started.

"He was on his way home," Mary continued. "He was trying to beat the rain, so he took a shortcut through the park on his way home."

"And Courtney just happened to be at the wrong place at the wrong time," he said.

"This was a crime of opportunity," Mary agreed. "But now we are two steps closer to finding him because we know Courtney knew him, and we know he lived near the park."

Chapter Thirty-three

The afternoon was dragging, as Friday afternoons generally do. But this was worse. Mary felt stuck at her office. She didn't want to go home, didn't want to be waiting at the house when Clarissa got home, didn't want to have to deal with all of the drama and confusion. She just felt overwhelmed, tired and emotional.

She reached over to the box of cookies she had purchased at lunch and was surprised to find that all of them were gone. *I just ate a dozen double chocolate macadamia nut cookies*, she scolded herself. *I disgust myself.*

Sighing, she pulled Courtney's file in front of her again, trying to see if there was anything she'd missed. The words swam in front of her eyes. *What is wrong with me?*

The ringing phone postponed the answer to that question as Mary eagerly answered it. "Mary O'Reilly Alden," she said.

"Hey, sweetheart, how are you doing?" Bradley asked.

Oh, I'm great, she replied silently. *I'm trying to double my clothing size in a week.*

"I'm good," she actually said out loud. "I've just been going over the reports again."

"Good, so you're busy?" he asked.

"Yes, really busy," she lied.

"So you wouldn't mind if I picked up Clarissa at school?"

A broad grin spread across her face. "No. No, I don't mind at all," she said. "And you know, maybe you need a daddy-daughter date. She really seems to be missing you."

"I guess I could take her out for ice cream," he pondered.

"And a movie," Mary interjected. "You could go out to a movie. Unless, of course, you have to work."

"No, I've actually got to run over to her school and meet with the principal before the end of the day," he said. "But then I've done all I can do. I have my officers still working on the case, but I decided I needed to spend some time with my family."

"Oh, well, wonderful," Mary said. "You and Clarissa make an evening of it."

"Are you sure you don't want to come?"

"I am positive," she said. "I'll go home and maybe take a bath and do my nails. Just have a little me time."

"You deserve a little me time," Bradley said. "And then, once Clarissa and I get home and she goes to bed, we can have a little us time."

Mary grinned. "I love us time," she said, her voice softening into a seductive whisper. "I'll be waiting for you."

"I'll be sure it's a short movie," he replied.

She laughed. "Take your time," she said. "Anticipation always makes things better."

Chapter Thirty-four

Bradley had to wipe the silly smirk off his face before he left his office. He knew he was stupid-in-love, but he didn't need to let all of his staff know it too. "Dorothy, I'm heading over to Lincoln Douglas School," he said. "After that I have a very important daddy-daughter date. But if you need me…"

"Chief, I think Freeport can let you have one night off," she said. "Besides, don't you have a new wife at home?"

Bradley couldn't help the grin that spread across his face. "Yeah, I do."

"I see," Dorothy said, not bothering to hide her smile. "I'll be sure no one bothers you after nine o'clock."

His grinned widened. "Thanks, Dorothy. Thanks a lot."

Pulling his cruiser up near the front of the school, Bradley waited at the glass door to be "buzzed in" by the office. He glanced at his watch and realized that if he didn't want to be blocked in by a dozen school busses, he needed to be quick. Once he was inside, he crossed the hall to the office. "Hi, Pam," he said to the receptionist. "I need a minute or two with Sandy and then I'd like to pick up Clarissa a little early."

"Sandy's waiting for you," Pam replied, pointing in the direction of the principal's office. "And I can call down to Clarissa's teacher and have her send Clarissa down with her backpack and coat."

"That would be great," Bradley said. "Thanks."

He knocked on Sandy's door and was invited in immediately. Not bothering to take a seat, he leaned against the doorframe and greeted the middle-aged black woman with a smile. "I just wanted to let you know that I reviewed the letter you composed about the missing girl," he said. "It's great and it really details how parents can help keep their children safe. I was hoping you'd let me bring it over to Julie at the district office and let her spread it throughout the other schools."

"You know you didn't have to ask me," Sandy said. "I'm fine with that. Actually, I'm fine with anything that helps keep our kids safe. Are there any leads?"

"Not yet," Bradley said. "But we're working on a couple of things."

"Good. I pray you find him before another child gets snatched," she said.

"Me too, Sandy," he replied. "Me too."

"Well, try and have a good weekend, Bradley," she said. "Remember, you have a lot of blessings in your life."

He straightened and nodded. "I do indeed," he said. "And you have a good weekend too."

Sandy looked beyond him through the glass windows into the school office. "Well, just look who's getting out of school a little early," she said, winking at Bradley. "I won't keep you."

"Thanks again," he said.

He stepped out of the office and nearly ran into Ray Giles, the truant officer he met at the school district meeting. He smiled and extended his hand. "Ray. Ray Giles. Right?" he asked, shaking the older man's hand.

Ray smiled back at him. "You're good with names and faces," he said. "If you ever decide to give up police work, you'd be a great truant officer."

Bradley laughed. "Thanks, I'll keep that in mind."

"Daddy!" Clarissa called, running across the office and throwing her arms around her father.

Bradley bent down and gave her a hug. "Hi, sweetheart, how was your day?"

Clarissa turned, smiling at the man standing next to her father and froze.

"Clarissa, what's wrong?" Bradley asked.

"This is your daughter?" Ray said, meeting Clarissa's eyes. "Well, I'm sure I'll never find her skipping school, will I?"

Leaning back against her father, she shook her head. "No," she stammered. "I would never, ever leave school without permission."

He bent down and stroked her cheek. "I didn't think so," he said, then straightening he returned his gaze to Bradley. "Have a nice weekend, Chief Alden."

Bradley nodded. "You too, Ray," he said, watching the man walk slowly down the school hallway.

Turning to Clarissa, he was ready to ask her about her reaction when Pam came up behind them. "You've got about two minutes before the buses get here," she said. "You better get while the getting's good."

"Thanks, we will," he said, grabbing her backpack and leading Clarissa out the door, the concern about her reaction slipping from his mind. "Guess what? We're going to have a date tonight."

Chapter Thirty-five

Ray Giles walked down the hallway feeling like an executioner was right behind him. All that little brat had to do was tell her daddy about the offered ride and the suspicion would all shift in his direction. If things weren't so hot right now, he could just say he was going to bring her back to school. But there was too much risk, and he was a guy who hated risk.

He slipped out the side door of the school and hurried to his car. He would have to take care of the little girl, but that wasn't going to happen until she was away from her daddy. Slipping into the car, he started to turn the key when he looked down at the passenger's seat and spied a memo from the superintendent. He really hated that jerk.

He started to turn the key and froze once again. A smile spread across his face. *Yeah, all I need is a little diversion*, he thought. *All I need is for them to find the bad guy and then I'm home free. Find the little girl, find her with the superintendent and problem's solved.*

He sighed as he finally turned the car on and backed out of the parking space. *Too bad she has to die so soon. I haven't even gotten to the fun part yet.*

Picking up his cell phone, he placed a quick call and put the phone on speaker. The phone rang three times before there was an answer.

"Dr. Sears."

"Dr. Sears, it's Ray Giles. I was just over at Lincoln Douglas dropping off my report and I saw Chief Alden there. He was asking questions about you."

"What?" Nick Sear's voice rang with fear. "He's got no business asking any questions about me."

"Doesn't your wife work there?" Ray asked, already knowing the answer.

"Yes, she does," he replied. "But there is nothing... He didn't talk to her, did he?"

"Well, I'd like to tell you all I know, but I'm afraid I might be overheard," he said. "I don't want you to get in trouble. You're my boss. You're a good boss. Maybe we could meet somewhere, and I could tell you what I heard."

"I can come to your place," Nick suggested.

Ray grinned; this couldn't be much better.

"Yeah, well, I don't think that's a great idea," he said. "I've noticed some cop cars swinging by my place. I think they've got us all under investigation."

Nick was breathing heavy. Ray could picture him wiping the sweat off his brow.

"Okay, I've got this other place," Nick finally said. "But you've got to swear that you won't tell anyone else about it."

Ray nearly laughed out loud. *Oh, yeah, doctor, your little love shack that I knew about four years ago. Sure, I won't tell anyone about it.*

"Of course I won't tell anyone," Ray replied. "I told you, I'm on your side. I wouldn't have called you if I wasn't."

Nick gave Ray the address to a small house on the edge of town. "I'm leaving now," Nick said. "Be there in fifteen minutes."

"I still have a couple more stops to make," Ray lied. "But I can be there in forty-five minutes. Besides, it will be less suspicious if you're there first and then I come much later."

"Oh, okay, that's true. I'll see you in forty-five minutes."

"Does this place have a garage?" Ray asked, knowing full well it did.

"Yes, it does. Why?"

"Leave the garage door open for me," Ray said. "I'll park my car in the garage, in case anyone drives by; they won't know we're meeting."

"Oh, that's a good idea," Nick said. "I'll open it when I get there. Don't be late."

"Oh don't worry," Ray said. "I'm treating this like my life depends on it."

Chapter Thirty-six

"Hey, you've barely touched your hamburger and fries," Bradley said to Clarissa, as they sat in a booth at one of her favorite fast-food restaurants. "Something wrong?"

Grabbing several fries and stuffing them into her mouth, she shook her head. "No," she muttered.

"Good. I'm glad because I really want our date to be special," he said. "Do you know this was Mary's idea? She thought it would be great for us to spend some time together."

Clarissa sighed and bit another French fry. *Really? I am going to have to listen to him talk about Mary all night.* She thought about it for a moment. *Maybe this is my chance to set things straight.*

"She just thought of it because she doesn't want to spend time with me," she said. "She really hates me."

Bradley put his own hamburger down on the plate and shook his head. "She does not hate you," he insisted. "I don't know where you got such an idea."

Shrugging, Clarissa picked up her own burger and took a bite. "I can just tell," she said. "I think it would be much better if you weren't married to her."

"What?" Bradley exclaimed, trying to remain calm. "Mary and I are not going to get a divorce."

Clarissa dropped her hamburger and looked up at Bradley. "But what if you found out she really did hate me?" she demanded. "What if you found out she's only nice to me when you're around? What would you do then?"

"If I found out those things," he said calmly, "– and I don't believe for one minute they are true – but if in some weird universe that were true, then I would insist we all go to family counseling so we could work things out."

She exhaled angrily. *Didn't he get it?*

"What if she didn't want to go to family counseling?" she asked. "What if she thought that was a stupid idea?"

"Mary wouldn't think it was a stupid idea," he said. "She loves me and she loves you. So she would put effort into making our new family work."

"But what if she didn't want to be married to you anymore?" she insisted. "What if she didn't want to be my mom? What if she didn't want any obligations?"

Bradley sat back against the booth and folded his arms over his chest. "Clarissa, you are my daughter. I searched for you for eight years. Mary not only helped me find you, she also helped us capture the man who killed your father and was trying to take you," he said. "She has done nothing but love you and treat you like her daughter. She has done nothing but try her best to be your mother. I don't understand why you are trying to make all of this so difficult."

Clarissa allowed tears to pool in her eyes and watched with guilty pleasure as Bradley's stern demeanor melted. "Clarissa, sweetheart, I just want you to understand…"

"If she hated me, who would you choose?" she asked tearfully.

"What?"

"If Mary said it's either me or her; which would you choose?"

"She's not…"

"Which?" she demanded.

"Well, since you are a little girl and you are my daughter and my responsibility, I suppose I would have to choose you," he said. "But that's just not going to happen."

Picking up a napkin, Clarissa dabbed it delicately against her eyes, just like she saw them do on television. "Thank you, Dad," she said sweetly. "I feel much better now."

Chapter Thirty-seven

"Hey, sweetheart, how are you feeling?" Ray said softly to the little girl who lay sleeping on the bed in his basement. "Guess what? We're going for a little ride."

He unstrapped the heavy band that held the girl to the bed, lifted her lethargic body into his arms and carried her up the stairs into his living room. "I really meant to keep you longer," he said. "But I find it is necessary for you to graduate much sooner than I had anticipated."

She groaned softly and tried to struggle.

"Oh, thank you," he said. "I almost forgot."

He placed her on a recliner covered in plastic and shoved it back, so she was nearly lying flat. She tried to move, tried to scream, but the drug kept her just under the surface. Her mind was screaming, but her body would not respond.

"Hey, baby, I love that look of horror in your eyes," he said. "And if we had more time I'd take one more go at you. But we got someone we've got to meet."

He grabbed a handful of hair, yanked her head back and then forced the vile-tasting liquid down her throat. "This should do it, baby," he said. "This should make you close your eyes and go to sleep forever."

After stuffing the empty bottle in his pocket, he picked her up, flung her over his shoulder and carried her out to the garage. "Sorry, the trunk's not too comfortable," he said. "But don't worry; it's going to be a short ride."

Covering her up with an old blanket, he slammed the trunk down and smiled. "You are about to meet your superintendent," he said. "Please remember that's he's a doctor, so be impressed."

He turned away from the car and looked around the garage, tapping his forefinger on his chin. "How to do it? How to do it?" he mused as he studied the boxes on the shelves.

He walked forward, pulled out a small box and opened it. Inside was a dangerous-looking hunting knife. He studied it for a moment and then shook his head. "Too messy."

Sliding the box back in place, he pulled out a bin filled with chemicals for the garden. "This could work," he said. "But men don't generally poison themselves."

Finally he pulled out an old cardboard box. He lifted the top and inside was an assortment of rope. The largest was a coil of thick manila rope about twenty feet long. He lifted the rope, testing the feel in his hand. "Yes, this could do the trick," he decided, stroking his hand along the rough surface. "Neat and believable."

He threw the rope into the back of his car and then went back into his house. Jogging back down to the basement, he opened the door to a small bathroom and entered the room. Over the sink was an old medicine cabinet with a mirror whose silver was beginning to wear, creating black spots across the front. The cabinet itself was rusted and looked unused. Ray opened the door to reveal a shiny, stainless steel interior that was not only refrigerated, but also had an inside light. On small glass shelves were a variety of small vials. Sorting through the vials, he finally picked the one he was looking for. He stuffed the vial in his pocket, opened a drawer in the vanity below the mirror and retrieved a hypodermic needle. "I hope the doctor doesn't mind mixed drinks," he said with a short laugh.

Whistling to himself, he hurried to the garage, backed the car out and drove casually down the driveway to the street. As the gates slowly opened, a neighbor walked by with her dog. Ray rolled down the window and waved to the woman. "Lovely day, isn't it?" he questioned.

"Oh, yes, spring is in the air," she agreed. "Will you be planting any more of your lovely pine trees soon?"

Shaking his head, his smile was a bit sad. "I had plans for a new one," he said. "But it seems I might have to delay things until later on in the year."

"Oh, well, that's such a shame," she said. "I do hope your plans for the next one work out."

Ray smiled at her. "Thank you, so do I."

He pulled out to the street, closed the gates behind him and drove through town to the address Nick had given him. As promised, the garage door was open and Ray drove right into the garage and turned his car off. He slipped on a pair of transparent latex gloves before leaving the car, then he walked over to the remote on the wall and pressed the button to close the large garage door. "Let the games begin," he whispered to himself as he turned the knob to let himself into the house.

Chapter Thirty-eight

Soft music was already playing in the background as Mary lit the scented candles she had placed around the room. She inhaled the patchouli, lavender and jasmine scent and hoped, as the salesclerk at the candle store promised, they would infuse sensuality into the air. She grinned as the promised scenario played out in her mind. *Bradley wanders into the room, exhausted from his work day and the date with Clarissa. He looks at me, an apology on his lips; he is just too tired tonight. Then, suddenly, he sniffs the air and, after a moment, sniffs it again. Inhaling deeply, filling his lungs with the perfume from the candles, his eyes widen at first and then lower seductively as his demeanor turns predatory. He is the wolf and I am his mate. He rushes across the room and pulls me into his arms. "I don't know what's come over me, Mary," he whispers, "but suddenly I'm infused with passion."*

Rolling her eyes and laughing out loud, Mary was a little startled when the bedroom door opened and Bradley walked in. "What's so funny?" he asked.

Walking over to him, she wound her arms around his neck and reached up for a soft kiss. "Oh, nothing," she said, slipping her arms down and loosening his tie. "How was your date?"

He sighed and held her for a moment. "It was…interesting," he said, bending down and kissing her neck. "I'm afraid her head is filled with all kinds of strange ideas."

She arched her head back, enjoying his caresses. "We'll just have to be patient with her," she said, as she closed her eyes in pleasure. "Her little world has been turned around so many times. It's not surprising she's confused."

He continued to nibble on her neck, working his way down to her collarbone, when he stopped. "Mary," he asked. "What's that weird smell?"

"Weird smell?" she murmured, still caught in the spell of his kisses.

He lifted his head and sniffed, then, after a moment, sniffed again. "Yeah, it kind of smells like mold."

Her passion banked, Mary looked up at him in disbelief. "Really? Mold?" she asked. "That's what you get from that scent?"

He sniffed again. "Yeah, mold and…funky perfume."

She stepped out of his arms and placed her hands on her hips. "It was supposed to infuse the room with sensuality."

Looking down at Mary dressed in black lace and satin, her hair down around her shoulders, her ivory skin soft and scented, and her hands on her hips in a stance of aggravation, Bradley decided he had never seen anything as sexy. He slowly took a step forward, placed his hands on her waist and deliberately pulled her against him. Bending his head, he whispered softly into her ear, "You infuse this room with sensuality. I don't need anything else."

"Good answer," she stammered, and leaned against him as her knees turned to water.

He continued to kiss her, nibbling on the sensitive areas around her neck, earlobe and collarbone. She moaned softly and he covered her mouth with his lips, taking them both even deeper into the passionate spell he was weaving.

She felt his arms slip around her and suddenly she was weightless, moving across the room in his arms. She felt the cool smoothness of their sheets underneath her heated back as she sunk into the mattress with Bradley above her. This was perfect. This was what she had been waiting for. This was…

"Daddy!"

The scream seemed to erupt from right outside their door.

"What the hell?" Bradley grumbled, rolling off Mary and walking across the room to the door.

He cracked the door open a few inches, angling his body so Mary was hidden from view. "What's wrong, Clarissa?" he asked the child standing right outside his bedroom.

"I had a bad dream," she said, a slight smile on her face.

Bradley stared at his daughter, noting the wide-eyed face, the perfectly brushed hair and the unrumpled pajamas. She had not been asleep at all. She was purposely trying to interrupt any private time he and Mary wanted to enjoy. "Go to bed, Clarissa," he said pointedly. "Now."

Her smile dropped. "But...but I was scared," she stammered.

"Go to bed," he repeated.

"But there were monsters," she pleaded, "and they were in my closet."

"Mike," Bradley shouted.

Mike immediately appeared next to Clarissa. "Hey, what's up?" he asked, shooting Bradley a grin.

"Clarissa thinks there are monsters in her room," he said. "So I was wondering if you would mind keeping her company until she falls asleep." He glared at Clarissa. "Really asleep."

"But I don't want Mike," she pleaded. "I want you."

"Sorry, Clarissa," he said. "But right now Mary and I are having private time and we don't want to be disturbed, at all. Mike will be there to help you and protect you."

"But...but...but," she stammered.

"Now, Clarissa," he said impatiently. "Go to bed."

Closing the door sharply, he leaned back against it and looked at Mary. She was huddled under the covers, her back against the pillows, waiting for him.

"Are you okay?" she asked.

"She just lied to me," he said, running his hand through his hair. "I thought, you know, that maybe all of this was just a misunderstanding. But she lied; she didn't have a nightmare. She hadn't been asleep. She purposely wanted to pull me away from you."

Pushing the covers aside, Mary walked over to him and wrapped her arms around his waist. "She's just figuring things out, testing her limits and generally being an eight-year-old," Mary said. "The most important thing is that we show her that we are united and she can't break us apart. And we show her that we love her."

Wrapping his arms around her, he bent down and placed a kiss on the top of her head. "You're right," he said. "Thanks for being so patient with the situation."

She lifted her head and met his eyes. "Hey, she's my daughter too," she said adamantly.

She means it, he thought, as love and gratitude filled his heart. *Even after all of this, she still considers Clarissa to be her daughter too.*

He began to bend down and kiss her, but stopped halfway and sniffed.

"Bradley?" she asked.

"Shhhhh," he said and then he sniffed the air again.

He turned back to look at her, his eyes lowering slightly and a predatory gleam to his smile. "You know, this stuff must grow on you," he said softly, as he swung her up in his arms. "I suddenly feel quite infused with passion."

Chapter Thirty-nine

The streetlights were shining when Ray finally made it back to the garage. He kept the entrance way open, shining enough light into the space without attracting too much attention.

He popped the trunk of the car and lifted the girl into his arms. She was a lightweight compared to Nick. Although her body was still lethargic, it was pliable, so she wasn't dead yet.

That's okay, he decided. *It will just prove that he drugged her before he killed himself. Sets up the scenario even better.*

Kicking the door closed behind him, he carried the child through the house, trying to decide where it would be best to leave the body. He couldn't hide it too well – he did want the police to find her once they came looking for Nick. But, he reasoned, Nick was not a stupid man. He wouldn't have kept his victims in a place where they might have been discovered.

He paused with the girl in the front staircase. Nick's body was swinging from the stairwell, the end of the rope looped over one of the top banisters. His eyes now stared sightlessly at Ray, his face purple from lack of blood. It hadn't been easy to convince Nick to jump, even with the drugs swimming through his system. He finally had to toss him over the railing himself. Ray looked down to see the tops of Nick's shoes just skimming over the wood floor. "Good thing you're short," he muttered.

Moving past the dead man, he carried the girl up the stairs and peered into each of the rooms on the second floor. The first one was a normal bedroom, the second had been turned into an office, but the third room was little more than a closet. Ray stepped out of the room and looked around the hallway. *That doesn't make sense. The house goes on for several yards more. Why would there be only a closet in that space?*

He laid the child on the carpet in the hall and went back into the third room. The room was shaped in a short rectangle with a window off center on the outside wall. Rather than a curtain, as in the other rooms, this window had privacy shutters on it. A collection of boxes and plastic tubs sat of the floor, against the back wall.

Ray flicked on the light switch and a corner floor lamp turned on. *Odd*, he thought, *the rest of the rooms have ceiling lights.*

Kicking one of the boxes, he was surprised to discover it was empty. He kicked another, they were all empty. Pushing them out of the way, he examined the wall they were covering. Kneeling down, he looked at the floor. The carpeting was pushed down in front of the wall, like something heavy had rolled over it. He stood, placed his hands on the wall and pushed against it. Something clicked against the pressure and the wall sprung forward. Moving to the

170

edge, he pushed his fingers beneath the small crack and pulled. Like a giant door, the wall pulled away, exposing a hidden room.

Waiting until his eyes adjusted to the darkness, Ray looked around for another light switch and finally found one on the wall adjacent to the door. When he clicked it on, a burst of laughter escaped his lips. "Well, you little pervert," he said. "You just helped me create the perfect crime."

The walls of the room were covered in pornography. Some ripped from magazines and some, obviously, taken with his own camera. One small section was dedicated exclusively to child porn, with subjects as young as toddlers.

The room also housed a desk with a computer and a four-poster brass bed, complete with handcuffs hanging from each corner. "You are one sick creep," Ray muttered. "At least I was trying to teach them something."

Reaching into his pocket, he pulled out the suicide note he had insisted Nick draft and placed it on the desk next to the keyboard. Then he hurried back to the hall, picked up the little girl and brought her back into the room. Laying her on the bed, he rubbed the handcuffs on her wrists and ankles to add some of her DNA to the restraints.

Stepping back, he looked at the girl's body sprawled across the bed and the disgusting photos in the background. "Yeah, paints a pretty damning picture," he said. "Now all I have to do is take care of that Alden kid."

Chapter Forty

Mary groaned when the cell phone went off in the early hours of the morning. Her eyes still closed, she lifted her hand to slap the alarm clock off, but it just didn't seem to be working. Chuckling, Bradley gave her a quick kiss on the cheek and rolled out of bed. "Mary, it's my phone," he said. "Go back to sleep."

Mumbling something incoherent, she snuggled back into her pillow and tried to resume her dream.

"When did they find him?" Bradley's voice was tense and directed. "And the girl? How is she?"

Mary rolled over and sat up in bed. She exhaled with relief when she saw Bradley's slight smile. "Good," he said. "Is she at Freeport Hospital or did they airlift her to Madison?"

He nodded again, cradling the phone between his shoulder and his chin, while he pulled clothes out of his drawer. "Yeah, I can be there in twenty minutes," he said. "Thanks for the good news."

He clicked off the phone and turned to Mary. "They just found Nick Sears's body in a small house near Henderson Avenue," he said.

"Nick Sears is dead?" Mary asked, astonished.

"Hung himself. Left a note confessing to everything," Bradley replied, hurrying toward the bathroom.

Mary slid out of bed and followed him. "But Henderson is nowhere near the park," she said. "That doesn't make sense."

Bradley stepped under the flowing water of the shower. "Yeah, I know," he said. "But they also found the kidnapped girl in the house with him."

"Is she going to be okay?" Mary asked.

"She's been given some pretty heavy-duty drugs, but they think she'll be fine," he said. "They've airlifted her up to Madison so she can be seen by specialists."

Leaning back against the sink, Mary shook her head. "I just can't believe we were that far off," she said. "And I have to admit, it all seems too neatly wrapped up."

Stepping out of the shower, Bradley stood next to her and applied shaving cream. "Yeah, I'm right there with you," he said. "And Dr. Sears didn't seem like the suicide type. He thought much too much of himself."

"Well, if it was Sears, then the children of Freeport can rest easy," she said. "But I'm not going to say anything to Celia until you call, okay?"

He stopped shaving for a moment and met her eyes through the shower. "I'm sorry I have to rush away again," he said. "I really wanted to spend some more time with you this morning."

Smiling back at him, she shrugged. "I understand, it's the job."

"Yeah, well, I'm hoping the job will slow down a little so I can enjoy being a married man," he replied, shaving under his chin.

"I enjoyed you being a married man last night," she teased.

He grinned at her. "I just might have to quit my job and stay home full time," he said.

He wiped the remaining shaving cream from his face and turned to her. "So, what's your plan for today?" he asked.

"I suppose it depends on Clarissa," she replied. "If she's willing, I thought I'd take her shopping for shoes and spring clothes. If not, I might see if Rosie and Stanley would be willing to come by and keep an eye on her so I can do some grocery shopping."

"I could always shop," he said.

She leaned up and kissed him. "Yes, you could," she said. "But chips, chili and cookies are not a balanced diet. Now, you finish getting dressed and I'll get you some breakfast."

"Thanks."

She grabbed her robe, walked down the hall and peeked in on Clarissa. She was sound asleep. Mary smiled as she looked at her face, so innocent in her sleep. "Don't be fooled," Mike whispered, appearing behind her. "She's only smiling in her sleep because she's planning your demise."

Mary softly closed the door and shook her head. "Don't be silly," she said. "She's just confused."

"Yeah, they said that about Lizzy Borden too," he grumbled.

She stopped at the top of the stairs. "Come on, Mike," she said. "You are her guardian angel; you're supposed to be on her side."

"Okay, you're right," he said. "But I don't know what happened to the cute little kid we all liked a few weeks ago."

Mary started down the stairs. "You know, you're right," she said. "I wonder if Katie or Maggie can tell us if anything happened while she was staying with them."

"That makes sense," Mike agreed. "Maybe someone said something."

"I'll call Rosie and Stanley once I get Bradley on his way," she decided. "Then we can go over and talk to Katie and Maggie to see if they can shed any light on the situation."

Mike seemed to hesitate for a moment. "Mary, there's something I need to tell you."

"Mike, what's wrong?" Mary asked.

"There are rules with guardian angels," he said. "I'm not great with them; I'll be the first to admit that. But the one big rule is that we can't interfere when someone is making bad choices on purpose. I can't interfere with Clarissa's agency; I can't stop her from doing something she already knows in her heart is wrong."

"That doesn't make sense," Mary argued. "She's just a little girl."

"Mary, she's eight years old, almost nine," he said. "And she knows the difference between right and wrong. If angels were allowed to interfere and change the consequences of someone's choice, it wouldn't be fair."

"Can you tell her?" she asked. "Can you at least warn her before she makes the choice that she'll be on her own?"

"Yeah, I can do that," he agreed. "I don't know if it's part of the rules, but yeah, I'll be sure she knows."

"Well, let's just pray it never comes to that," Mary said.

Chapter Forty-one

The crime scene was abuzz with local law enforcement, news reporters and FBI agents. Bradley shook his head as he pulled his cruiser up to the curb. *This is a three-ring circus.*

Stepping out of the vehicle, he was immediately assailed by reporters. "Chief Alden, did you suspect Dr. Sears of kidnapping?"

Actually I only suspected him of being an ass, he thought. "No comment," he said, pushing through the crowd toward the house.

"Chief Alden, where do you think the other bodies are buried?"

"No comment," he repeated, still moving forward.

"Chief Alden, do you have the address for the parents of the kidnapped child?"

Bradley froze and stared at the young reporter who posed the question. "If I find out that you, any of you, have intruded on their privacy while their child hangs between life and death, I will arrest you for interfering with an ongoing criminal case," he said. "Do you understand me?"

The young reporter swallowed and nodded.

"Good," he said. "Listen, I know you want information and I am happy to share it with you. But let me take a look at what's going on inside, then I'll hold a press conference and give you all the details I can."

Not waiting for a response, he hurried to the house and closed the door behind him. He looked around quickly, noting that although the hedges around the windows were high, an enterprising reporter might be able to get a shot of the deceased. "Deutsch and Killoran," he called to two of his officers. "Would you make sure we have officers stationed around the circumference of the building to make sure no reporters cross the crime-scene-tape border? We don't want the interior of this house showing up on the six o'clock news."

Walking over to the coroner who was examining the body, Bradley waited as the man jotted down a few final notes and placed a covering over the body laid out on the hallway floor. "So, what do you think?" he asked.

Bradley liked the new coroner, Chris Malik, a retired country doctor, who shot straight from the hip and didn't worry about being politically correct. Chris scratched his head for a moment and then looked at Bradley. "Well, he's dead," he replied, and then he paused and popped a piece of chewing gum in his mouth. "Seems to me he could've found himself at least half a dozen easier ways to end his life."

Bradley looked up to the top of the staircase and nodded. "Yeah, I agree. He nearly didn't get the rope high enough."

"Yeah, would have been an awful mess if he just broke his ankle and then had to fall over to strangle himself. You'd think a doctor would have been smarter about that."

Obviously Chris had met the superintendent, Bradley decided.

Chris leaned back on his heels and rocked back and forth for a moment. "There's another thing that's strange," he said. "I took a look at the suicide note he left."

Bradley nodded. "It was read to me over the phone," he said. "Seemed pretty straightforward. He confessed to raping and killing all of the girls over the past ten years."

"Straightforward if you got the equipment," he replied.

"What do you mean by that?"

"I can pretty much guarantee that the fellow who wrote that suicide note is not the fellow laying on the floor in front of us," he stated positively.

"How do you know?"

"Chief Alden, when a coroner comes to the scene of a sexual crime, he has to take samples from various parts of the body," he explained simply. "Those aren't the usual parts we pay attention to, parts I'd rather not see, quite frankly. But we've got to swab 'em down for DNA and semen samples."

"Oh, okay, I understand what you're saying," he said. "You didn't find any evidence of sexual assault."

"No, I'm saying I didn't find any evidence of anything," he said.

"What?"

"Nick Sears wasn't just shooting blanks, he wasn't shooting at all. Didn't have a gun, if you know what I mean."

"He doesn't have a..."

"Clean gone," the doctor said. "Some kind of freak accident I suppose. But judging by the scar tissue, it happened when he was a youngster."

"So there's no way..."

"He raped anyone, not in this world," the doctor interrupted. "Of course, he could have assaulted them, but that's not what the suicide note says, and you'd think he be pretty clear in his suicide note."

Bradley shook his head. "With his condition, he probably was more comfortable watching and not participating."

"Probably why he got his kicks with his camera," Chris surmised.

"Well Chris, you just turned my suicide into a homicide," Bradley said with a sigh.

"Don't mention it, youngster," Chris said, patting Bradley's shoulder. "Don't mention it at all."

"Speaking of don't mention it," Bradley said, lowering his voice. "How long can you keep this information on ice? I've still got a killer out there who thinks he's pulled a fast one."

"I can keep it quiet for a couple of days," he said. "But it's not me you've got to worry about.

Once this hits the press, his good wife is going to probably talk about his lack of family jewels to clear his good name."

"Crap, you're right," Bradley replied. "Well, we've got to move fast. Thanks Chris."

He looked around and saw that Ashley Deutsch was in the house. "Hey, Ashley, find his cell phone," he said. "We need to find out who he talked to last night."

"We've been looking for his phone, Chief," she replied. "And we can't find it."

Bradley thought for a moment. "Call Julie Quinn from the school district, ask her about the carrier the school district uses and what Sears's phone number was. Then call the carrier and get a print out."

"On it," Ashley responded.

"Killoran," Bradley called, when the officer entered the house. "I need you to get a female officer, drive out to Sears's house and stay with his wife. I don't want the press to get anywhere near her. Got it?"

"Yes, sir," he said, and he turned and hurried from the house.

"Now all we can do is wait for a break," Bradley muttered under his breath.

Chapter Forty-two

"Clarissa," Mary called up the stairs. "Rosie and Stanley are here to visit with you. I'll only be gone a little while and then we can talk about shopping again."

There was no response from Clarissa and Mary sighed. "I hope she comes down once I leave," she said. "I'm not her favorite person right now."

Rosie gave Mary a hug. "Give her some time," she said. "She's going through a lot."

"Iffen I acted like that, I'd be seeing the business end of a paddle," Stanley said, taking off his coat and hanging it over the chair. "Folks are way too soft with children today."

"Stanley, my mom paddled my brothers and me when we were growing up," Mary said. "But it was only when we did something that could have endangered our lives. She wanted to be sure the lesson sunk in." She rubbed her backside. "And it always did. But Clarissa is more confused about how she fits into our new family and I think spanking her would send the wrong message."

"Well, maybe you're right and maybe you ain't," he said, folding his arms over his chest. "But I gotta say that kids in my generation had a whole lot more respect for their elders than kids today."

"Yes, but I don't think you want children to blindly listen and obey to someone just because they are an adult, as we did," Rosie said, giving his arm a little squeeze. "The world today is too full of adults who mean to harm children. So children should learn that adults need to earn trust and respect, just like everyone else."

"Well, Mary should be respected," Stanley argued, nodding at Mary. "She's more than earned Clarissa's trust and respect."

"I don't think that's the problem," Mary said, pulling her coat out of the closet and slipping it on. "I think Clarissa is fearful; that's why I want to go over and speak with Katie and Maggie. Maybe they can give us a clue about what prompted her concerns."

"Well, you go and have a nice chat with the Brennans," Rosie said. "And I'm sure we will have a delightful time with Clarissa."

"Thanks," Mary said.

She reached for the doorknob just as her cell phone rang. Pulling it from her pocket, she answered it. "Hello."

"Mary, it's Celia. Is it true? Someone posted on Facebook that they found the man who kidnapped the last little girl."

Closing her eyes for a moment, Mary sighed softly. "Well, it's early yet in the investigation," Mary said. "But they did get a breakthrough."

"Mary, please, can't you give me any more information?" Celia pleaded. "I'm going a little crazy."

"Sure, why don't we meet at my office," she said. "I can be there in ten minutes."

"Thank you, Mary. I'll be there."

Mary hung up her phone and turned to Rosie and Stanley. "Change of plans," she said. "I need to meet a client at my office. I shouldn't be very long."

"Don't matter to us," Stanley said. "You just go and do what you need to do. Rosie brought over stuff to make cookies, so I reckon Clarissa will be down those stairs soon as the cookies are out of the oven."

"You two are the best," Mary said, giving them each a hug. "I'll call Katie on the way over to my office and let her know I had to change plans."

Mike followed her out onto the porch. "I'll hang here," he said. "I want to keep an eye on Clarissa."

"Thanks, Mike," she agreed. "That would be great."

Chapter Forty-three

Ray Giles sat in his car, watching Mary leave the house and drive away in her Roadster. He'd been there since dawn, about a half block away from the house, waiting for his opportunity to take the little Alden girl for a nice long ride. He'd seen Chief Alden leave in the early morning hours and knew they had found Nick's body. Smiling to himself, he settled back in the seat. It was only a matter of time before everything was tied up in a neat bow.

He gazed up into the rearview mirror at the small potted pine tree sitting in the back seat. He had picked it up that morning at the twenty-four-hour, big-box store's garden center. One more pine tree, one more student and then he would have to leave Freeport. Even though he'd thrown them off his trail, he realized that he was going to have to find a new town with new students for his special school. The little Alden girl would have to be placed on an accelerated plan; he needed to have the new young pine planted by tomorrow morning, just before he left town.

Tapping his fingers on the steering wheel, he wondered how long he was going to have to wait. Even though he didn't consider the elderly couple much trouble, there would be a risk with having two of them in the house. And since it was a Saturday, he couldn't use his customary ploy of truancy. He sighed; he was just going to have to sit back and wait.

Suddenly, an explosion of noisy children emerged from the house he was parked across from. *The Brennan clan*, he thought, *those boys were always stirring up trouble.*

He watched the youngest, a little girl, follow her brothers down the steps. *Why does she look familiar? Oh, yes, she was with the Alden girl that morning. She was the one who pulled her back away from the street.*

"I'm going to go see if Clarissa wants to play," she called to her brothers and started to run down the street.

Smiling and skipping, she was lost in her own world, when she suddenly froze and turned to look at Ray's car. He rolled down the window and smiled at her. "Hello there," he said. "I'm just waiting for a friend to come out of their house. Don't I know you?"

Her eyes filled with fear and she kept transferring her gaze between his face and the back of his car. Finally, she took several slow steps backward, turned and ran back to her house.

"Hey, I thought you were going to go get Clarissa," one of her brothers called.

"I just remembered," she called back as she ran up the porch steps. "She can't come out and play today."

Ray watched her run into the house, slamming the door shut behind her and a knot of fear twisted in his stomach. *She knew*, he thought. *Somehow she knew about my students.*

Turning the car on, he casually pulled out of the parking spot and drove down the road. Now he was going to have to rely on the small GPS tracker he placed on Clarissa's backpack when he saw her at the school. Turning the locater on, he saw the red dot remaining stationary at the location of her home. "Still working," he said softly. "Now, come on Clarissa; it's a beautiful day to take a walk. I'll be waiting."

Chapter Forty-four

Celia rushed through the door of Mary's office a moment after Mary had arrived. "What did they find?" Celia asked, her words spilling out of her mouth. "Did they find anyone else? Have they located the bodies? Are they sure this is the right person?"

"Just wait a minute, Celia," Mary said. "Have a seat and I'll tell you what I know. Okay?"

Celia took a deep breath and then collapsed into a chair. "I just want it to be..." she said, her voice trembling. "I just need it to be over."

Mary sat on the edge of her desk in front of Celia's chair. "What I'm going to tell you needs to stay confidential," she said. "At least until the press gets a hold of it."

"Okay, I promise," Celia replied. "I'll keep it to myself."

"Bradley was concentrating on members of the school district," Mary explained, "because it seemed the kidnappings were linked to the attendance and truancy records."

"I hadn't even thought of that," Celia said, shaking her head in awe. "And Ray Giles, the truancy officer, is a good friend of ours. He would have helped me with research."

"Well, Bradley hadn't gotten very far in his investigation when he received a call this morning. Nick Sears killed himself last night and the young girl who had been kidnapped was found in his home."

Celia clapped her hands over her mouth. "Oh, I read they had found her," she said. "Is she going to be…?"

"She's alive, but in critical condition," Mary said. "She had a lot of drugs pumped into her system."

"Nick Sears," Celia repeated. "I would have never considered him."

"Well, the case hasn't been closed yet," Mary said, still feeling uncomfortable with the outcome.

"But if he killed himself and left a note, really, what else can there be?"

"You'd think that would be open and shut, wouldn't you?" Mary mused.

"But you don't think so."

Shrugging, Mary stood up and walked to the other side of the desk. "Maybe I'm just looking for shadows when there aren't any," she said. "The house where he had her was on Henderson; that wasn't close to the park at all."

"And Courtney didn't know Dr. Sears," Celia added.

"What?" Mary asked.

"Courtney didn't know Dr. Sears," Celia repeated. "She wouldn't have carried on a conversation with him."

189

"Celia, would you mind if I shared that with Bradley?"

"No, please do," she said. "I want the right person caught, not the convenient one."

"Me too," Mary agreed.

Celia stood up and walked with Mary to the door. "Call me when you find out the truth," she said.

Mary nodded. "I promise," she said. "First thing."

Chapter Forty-five

As Mary drove home, she called Bradley. "Hi, how's it going?" she asked.

"I can't say a lot," he said. "But I can say a lot has changed since I left home this morning."

"I just met with Celia," Mary said. "She read the news on Facebook."

"Good grief," Bradley said. "What did she read?"

"Just that the little girl was recovered and on her way to the hospital," Mary said. "No other details."

Mary turned on Empire toward her house. "But I wanted to let you know that Courtney did not know Nick Sears," Mary said. "Celia said she would not have gotten into a car with him."

"Yeah, that matches with some of the stuff we've discovered," he said. "Looks like another long day. Are you okay?"

She smiled. "Yes, I'm fine," she said. "I'm heading home. I'm anxious to see what Rosie and Stanley have got planned with Clarissa."

"Well, call me if you need me," he replied. "Love you."

"Love you too," she said. "See you later."

She hung up the phone and turned into her driveway, a little surprised to see smoke coming out of the chimney. The weather hadn't really been cold enough to light a fire lately. Grabbing her purse, she hurried across the lawn and up the stairs to the door.

Opening the door, she found Stanley and Rosie adding logs to an already roaring fire. "Hi," she said, stepping in and removing her coat. "What's going on?"

"Well, Clarissa thought it would be a great surprise to help you clean up your cabinets," Rosie said, with a bright smile on her face. "So she suggested we start a fire and burn up some old papers you wanted to destroy."

"Old papers?" Mary asked.

"Yeah, she said there was a box of old stuff in the cabinets you didn't want to keep," Stanley added. "Just old junk."

"My box?" Mary cried, running into the kitchen. "Clarissa, please tell me…"

Clarissa stood on the countertop, holding Mary's keepsake box upside-down in her hands. She turned as Mary ran into the room, and fear washed over her face. "I didn't mean to," she yelled.

The floor was coated with thin slippery paper and, before Mary realized it, she was sliding on the floor, her feet slipping out from underneath her. She grabbed wildly for something to hold onto, but her fall was too fast and there was nothing nearby. She fell backward and felt her head make contact with the edge of the butcher-block counter and then there was nothing but darkness.

Chapter Forty-six

"Mary!" Clarissa screamed, scrambling down from the countertop. "Mary, are you okay?"

"Oh, Stanley," Rosie shrieked. "She's bleeding. Mary's bleeding."

"Go to the fridge and grab some ice," Stanley yelled, grabbing a dishcloth from the sink. "We got to stop the flow of blood."

He looked up at Clarissa. "You know how to call 911?" he asked sharply.

She nodded.

"Well, then call them, so your new mom don't die," he yelled.

Sobbing, Clarissa grabbed the phone in the living room and dialed 911. "My mom fell," she cried. "She fell and she's bleeding and she's not awake."

Rosie brought the ice over in a plastic bag and Stanley gently placed it on Mary's head, trying to staunch the flow of blood with the dishcloth.

"Oh, Stanley, is she going to die?" Rosie asked.

Stanley started to reassure Rosie, but saw that Clarissa was also listening. "I don't know," he said. "Falls like these can kill people."

"The ambulance is coming," Clarissa sniffed. "I told them to come fast."

Mike appeared in the midst of the chaos. "What happened?" he asked Clarissa.

"I did it," she cried. "I was going to burn Mary's stuff, her special stuff, and she came into the room and slipped on the papers and hit her head. She's not waking up, Mike. She's going to die and it's my fault."

Clarissa ran from the room and up the stairs to her bedroom, slamming the door firmly behind her.

Stanley looked up in the direction Clarissa had been speaking. "Mike, iffen you're still here, don't worry," he said. "She's got a nasty bump, probably a concussion, and head wounds always bleed a lot. But I have a feeling she's going to be just fine."

But Mike wasn't standing where Clarissa left him, he was on the floor kneeling next to Mary and talking to her. "Hey, babe, you got to hang in there," he said. "I know it would be easy to let go, easy to just walk away, but you've got to fight and you've got to stay. It would ruin Clarissa's life to know that her actions killed her mother. And Bradley, how would he go on knowing that his daughter killed you? Babe, I know you want to be with me. I know I'm irresistible, but you made a commitment and you gotta hang tough for a while."

Leaning over, he placed a kiss on Mary's forehead. "Come on, babe, take a deep breath and grab back on to your body."

Mary groaned slightly and Stanley breathed a sigh of relief. "I think she's gaining consciousness."

"There you go," Mike said. "I always knew you were a scrapper, Mary. Besides, you've got more to fight for than you realize."

Mary blinked and looked up at Stanley. "What happened...?" she started and then she winced in pain. "Owwww, I feel like I was hit in the head with a semi."

"Pretty close," Rosie said, dabbing the tears from her eyes. "You got hit with a butcher-block counter."

"Who threw it?" she whispered.

"You kind of threw yourself against it," Stanley said. "And you weren't very graceful in the execution."

"Blame my dad," she whispered. "He never let me take ballet lessons."

The sounds of the siren came up the street and stopped in front of their house. Mary tried to turn her head and nearly screamed. "Please, Stanley, not an ambulance," she said. "I really hate ambulances. I really hate hospitals. I die in hospitals."

Mike leaned over and smiled at her. "You won't die in this one," he said. "I promise. Now do as you're told and I'll come along for the ride."

"Promise?" she asked.

He nodded. "Yeah, I promise."

"I ain't promising nothing," Stanley grumbled. "You're going to that hospital and that's that."

Rosie hurried to the door and let the paramedics in.

"She fell backward against the edge of the counter," Stanley explained. "She's got quite a large knot on her head and she lost consciousness for about five minutes."

"It would be best for her to go into the emergency room," the paramedic stated. "They can check her for concussion and maybe perform a CT scan to see if there is any internal damage. Does one of you want to ride along?"

"Rosie you stay here with Clarissa and I'll go in the ambulance with Mary, okay?" Stanley asked.

Rosie nodded. "Please call me and let me know everything's okay."

They carefully loaded Mary onto the gurney, carried her out of the house and into the waiting ambulance. Stanley rode up front, next to the driver, and Mike stayed next to her in the back with the other paramedic.

"Hey, how are you doing?" he asked.

"My head really hurts," she replied.

"Yes, ma'am, I'm sure it does," the paramedic replied. "But don't worry, we'll be at the emergency room in just a minute."

"Oh, goodie," Mary muttered.

"That's my girl," Mike chuckled. "Miss Mary Sunshine."

Chapter Forty-seven

Clarissa was curled up on her bed, sobbing. She kept seeing Mary lying on the floor with blood all around her. She hadn't been moving. Just like her mom at the bus station. Maybe Mary was already dead, but no one would tell her. She killed Mary, just like she killed her dad and mom. Mrs. Gunderson was right, she was nothing but trouble.

She took a deep shuddering breath and sat up on the bed. Pulling a few tissues from the box on the nightstand, she wiped her eyes and nose. She had to decide what to do next. Even if Mary wasn't dead, she knew they wouldn't want her anymore. She had wanted to make Mary not want to be married to Bradley anymore; she had wanted Mary to be angry with her.

But she remembered the look on Mary's face when she came into the kitchen. It wasn't anger; she was sad. She looked at Clarissa and she was sad. Clarissa had been ready to yell at Mary. She had been ready for Mary to yell back and tell her she didn't want her to be her daughter anymore. But she didn't think Mary would be sad.

I should be the one who's dead, Clarissa thought. *Then I wouldn't be a problem at all.*

She slid off her bed and walked over to her nightstand, opened the top drawer and pulled out the photo Bradley had given her. He found it in her old house when he was trying to find her and her mom. The photo showed Clarissa with her mom and dad. They were laughing together. Another tear slid down her cheek. *That's where I belong*, she thought, *with my mom and dad in heaven.*

Remembering Maggie's suggestion about finding her dad at her old house, she had an idea. Maybe her dad could take her to heaven with him. Maybe they could just carry her up through the stars and she wouldn't ever have to worry about being alone again. She could just be with her mom and dad.

She looked down into the drawer and saw the sliver of china from Mary's chest. Putting the photograph down, she carefully picked the china up, tenderly held it and rubbed the smooth side. Another tear ran down her cheek as she remembered Mary giving it to her. She remembered how Mary had hugged her, even after she had broken it. Maybe Mary had loved her after all.

Taking another deep breath, she put the sliver back in the drawer and closed it. It was too late now. Mary was probably dead and Bradley would be angry with her. She paused in her thought process and shook her head. *No,* she thought, *he wouldn't be angry. He would be sad too.*

Picking up her backpack, she put the photo in it, and sliding the drawer back open, she pulled out the sliver of china and carefully placed it in an outside pocket. Then she packed up some of her clothes and tucked them tightly inside.

Looking around her room one last time, she sadly shook her head. *I need to go,* she thought. *They will be happier when I'm gone.*

Hitching her backpack onto her shoulder, she let herself out of her room and walked slowly down the stairs. Rosie was on her hands and knees cleaning up the blood on the kitchen floor. When she looked up at her, Clarissa could see that Rosie was still crying. *She must hate me too.*

"Clarissa," Rosie said, wiping her eyes with her handkerchief. "What do you need dear?"

"I, um," she swallowed because her throat felt tight. "The Brennans called and said I should go over there so you could go to the hospital and be with Mary."

"That's funny," Rosie said, getting to her feet. "I didn't hear the phone ring."

"I picked it up fast," Clarissa lied. "It probably didn't even ring downstairs."

"Well, let me get my coat and I'll walk you down," she said.

Clarissa shook her head. "That's okay, really," she said. "They're going to be watching for me."

She hurried to the closet and grabbed her coat, heading to the door. She grabbed a hold of the knob and started to twist it, and then she stopped and looked over her shoulder at Rosie. "Nana Rosie, could you do me a favor?" she asked.

"Sure, sweetheart, what do you need?"

"When you get to the hospital, will you please tell Mary that I love her and I'm sorry I made her sad," she said, fighting back her tears.

"Of course I will," she said. "And don't you worry, she'll be back from the hospital in no time, and you will all be one happy family again."

Clarissa nodded, opened the door and slipped out.

Chapter Forty-eight

Bradley looked down at his ringing cell phone, surprised to see the dispatcher's number appear. "Alden," he said.

"Hey, Chief, it's Jody. I thought I'd let you know we just received a 911 from your new address," she informed him. "A little girl called saying that her mom fell and she was bleeding and wouldn't get up. We've sent an ambulance and they're on their way to the hospital with a female adult."

Panic filled his heart and he forced himself to be calm. "Did they give you any more information?" he asked, already running out the door and heading to his car.

"She was responding, but she seemed to be having a conversation with someone who wasn't there," she said. "So they were concerned about hallucinations caused by a concussion."

He nearly laughed hysterically. *It must be Mike*, he thought.

"Thanks, Jody," he said. "I'm on my way to the hospital. Can you contact Ashley and let her know where she can reach me?"

"Sure thing, Chief," she said. "I hope she's okay."

Bradley started the cruiser and didn't think twice about turning on the sirens and speeding toward the hospital. *She hates hospitals.* The thought kept running through his mind. *I need to be there before she gets there.*

He pulled in right behind the ambulance and ran to the back door before they had it opened. "How is she?" he demanded.

The confused paramedic looked at the frantic Chief of Police. "I don't know if we can tell you..." he began.

"She's my wife, dammit," he growled. "So tell me how she's doing."

"I'm fine, Bradley," Mary said weakly, as the other paramedic opened the back doors. "Thanks for being here."

He ran to her side, took her hand in his and walked alongside the gurney. "Hey," he said softly, searching her for injuries. "Fancy meeting you here."

"Hey," she replied, taking a deep breath. "Do you know that more accidents happen in the home than anywhere else?"

"Really?" he asked, touching her face gently. "Well, then, where can we go to make sure you're safe all the time?"

The hospital doors slid closed behind her and she gripped his hand tighter. Then she looked over at Mike who was walking on the other side. "Don't leave me alone," she said to both of them.

"I right here with you, babe," Mike said.

"What he said," Bradley said, earning him a strange glance from the paramedics.

The emergency room doors opened and they were met by the attending physician. "I'm going to have to ask you to wait for her outside while I examine her," he said.

"Sorry, doctor," Bradley said. "She's under my protection and I have to be with her at all times."

"You tell him," Mike said. "We're like Secret Service. We really should have stopped to get some sunglasses."

Chuckling softly, Mary nodded, wincing at the pain. "He really needs to stay with me," she said.

He looked down and saw the fear in Mary's eyes and nodded, smiling down at her. "Okay, let's take you in exam room three and have a look at you."

"Thank you, doctor," she said.

A nurse followed them in and took her blood pressure and temperature, and then recorded them on her chart.

"So, can you sit up?" the doctor asked.

"Yes, I think so," Mary replied, trying to maneuver herself to a sitting position with Bradley's help.

Turning off the overhead light, the doctor shined a penlight in Mary's eyes and then away from them, then into them again. "Mmmm-hmmm," he muttered, turning on the light and jotting down notes.

He took a small rubber mallet from his pocket, tapped it against her knee and her knee jumped in response. "Mmmm-hmmm," he replied again.

Then he faced her. "So, I understand you blacked out," he said. "How long were you in that state?"

"I don't know," Mary replied. "I was unconscious at the time."

He grinned. "Obviously your verbal response and cognitive abilities are just fine."

"Why thank you, doctor," she said. "May I return the compliment?"

Chuckling, he jotted some notes down in her chart. "So, seriously, other than your head, what else hurts?" he asked.

"My lower back is pretty sore," she admitted. "I don't know if I hit something on the way down or I just tensed my muscles before I hit."

"How did the accident occur?"

"I was hurrying into the kitchen and didn't see a piece of paper on the floor," she said. "I slipped on the paper and tried to take out the edge of the butcher-block countertop."

"Ouch. Okay, let me take a look at your head."

He examined the bump on her head. He let out a slow whistle. "Well, you did a good job with this one. No wonder you're sore. I'd like to run some more tests just to be sure you don't have any internal injuries."

"What kind of tests?" Bradley asked.

"I'd like to do CT scan, just to rule out any internal head injury," he said. "And then, just to be sure there aren't any injuries to her kidneys, I'd like to do a urinalysis. The aching could simply be muscular, but I'd rather be safe than sorry."

"How long am I going to be here?" Mary asked.

The doctor smiled at her. "What, you're already tired of my amazing bedside repartee?" he asked.

"Nothing personal, but I have this thing about hospitals," she said.

"Let me see how quickly we can get those tests run and reviewed," he said. "And I'll get you out of here as quickly as possible."

"Thank you," she said. "I really appreciate it."

Chapter Forty-nine

Clarissa hurried around the side of the house and back through the yard to the alley. She didn't want to run the risk of anyone seeing her. She paused for a moment behind the garage. The afternoon sun was beginning to move toward the west and the sky was already beginning to darken. In a few hours it would be completely dark and cold. *I could stay*, she said to herself. *I could stay and see if Mary is okay.*

But what if she isn't okay? The unbidden thought crept into her mind. *What if Mary is in a coffin, just like my mother?*

The mental image of Mary lying lifeless in a wood coffin at the funeral home caused her to feel sick to her stomach. She looked at the house and shook her head. *They don't want me there anymore.*

Her head bent down, tears welling up in her eyes, Clarissa walked down the alley toward the next street. The only solution was to find her father. And the only place she would have a chance was at her old house, where Maggie said he might be.

"Hey, Clarissa, wait!"

Clarissa turned quickly to see Maggie riding down the alley on her bike toward her. "Where are you going?" she asked as she slid to a stop next to her.

"I can't tell you," Clarissa replied. "You need to go."

Maggie shook her head. "No, I'm not going to go until you tell me," she replied. "I can tell you've been crying. What happened?"

"I think I killed Mary," she whispered.

"What?" Maggie shouted, incredulous.

"It was an accident," Clarissa said, "but I caused it. She's at the hospital with Mike and Stanley."

"Are you going to the hospital?"

Wiping a sleeve over her teary eyes, she shook her head. "No, I'm going to my old house," she said. "I'm going to find my daddy."

She decided not to tell Maggie that she wanted to die and be with her parents. She knew it would just make Maggie upset. "I need to see if he'll talk to me," she said. "Maybe because I can see Mike, I'll be able to see him too."

"But you can't go by yourself," Maggie said. "I saw that man, the man with ghosts in his car, watching your house this morning. I think he wants to catch you."

A flutter of fear blossomed in Clarissa's chest, but she rejected it. "No, he won't try and get me," she said, "because I saw him at the school when my dad was there. He knows my dad is the police chief. And I know his name; it was on his tag. Ray Giles."

"But if you know his name, he might want to get you because he doesn't want you to tell it to your dad," Maggie argued.

"Maggie, I have to go," Clarissa said. "I just have to."

Maggie slid off the seat of her bike. "Then take my bike," she said. "So you can go faster."

"I can't take your bike," Clarissa said. "I don't know when I'll come back."

Shrugging, Maggie pushed the handlebars into Clarissa's hands. "That's okay," she said. "I can just use one of the boys' bikes if I need to. You take it, just in case."

Clarissa laid the bike on the ground and wrapped her arms around Maggie. "You are the best friend I ever had," she said.

"I wish you wouldn't go," Maggie said, hugging her friend back. "I wish you would just come to my house and we could figure everything out."

Shaking her head again, she stepped back and picked up the bike. "I can't, Maggie," she said. "I've done too much bad stuff. I have to go."

"My mom says when people love you, they forgive you for bad stuff if you're really sorry."

"I'm really sorry," Clarissa said, climbing on the bike. "But I don't think people love me enough for that."

She pushed down on the pedal and the bike started to move. "Goodbye, Maggie," she called and rode away from her friend.

208

Chapter Fifty

"How long does it take them to order a test?" Mary asked, laying on the bed in the emergency room. "I need to get home and make sure Clarissa knows I'm okay."

"Don't worry about Clarissa," Bradley said. "She and Rosie are probably baking you some get-well cookies."

Mary smiled. "You're probably right," she said. "I'm just a worry wart."

Bradley leaned over and kissed her forehead. "No, you're a mom," he said.

She smiled up at him. "Yes. Yes I am," she agreed. "So, tell me about the kidnapping case. Was Nick Sears the perp?"

Bradley sat down on a chair next to the bed and shook his head. "No, he's not," he said. "Chris, the coroner, found enough evidence to prove it was a homicide, not a suicide."

"So the kidnapper set him up?" Mary asked, amazed. "You must have been getting pretty close for him to do that."

"Yeah, that's what I'm afraid of," he said. "But we're not finding anything that points to a suspect."

"Last phone calls?" Mary asked.

Bradley smiled. "Yeah, even though his cell phone was missing, we were able to get a print out," he said. "The last calls were from Ray Giles and Julie said that it was routine for Giles to call him at the end of the day."

"Ray Giles," Mary said slowly. "You know, when I was with Celia today she mentioned him. She said he was a friend of the family. That she wished she had thought of the absences angle because he would have helped her."

"So, he's someone Courtney knew too," he surmised. "Someone she might have taken a ride from."

Mary nodded. "He had access to the records. Heck, he's driving around all day looking for kids as his job. He's got the perfect cover. Where does he live?"

Bradley reached for his phone and placed a call to Dorothy. After a few moments, he turned to Mary. "He lives on Woodside Drive, right behind the park."

"Bingo," Mary said.

"Yeah, I think you're right," he said. "As soon as we get you home, I'll get a search warrant, and we'll pay a little visit to Mr. Giles."

Chapter Fifty-one

The emergency room waiting room was fairly empty when Rosie walked through the entrance. The glass sliding doors slid closed behind her. She looked and saw Stanley snoozing in a corner chair and hurried over to sit next to him. "Stanley," she said, shaking his arm and waking him up. "How's Mary?"

Waking up with a start, he stared at her for a moment. "Why ain't you home with Clarissa?" he asked.

"The Brennans called and told Clarissa to come over to their place, so I could be here with you and Mary," she said.

"Well, that was nice of them," he said. "Bradley arrived at the hospital at the same time we did. He came out a little while ago and told me they were going to do a CT scan on her, just to make sure there's no internal damage. I'm thinking iffen she was in bad shape, there's no way he woulda left her side, even for a couple of minutes. So, I think she's gonna be just fine."

Rosie collapsed back against the chair. "Well, that's a blessing isn't it?" she said with relief. "After all that blood, and then she wouldn't wake up, I was so worried."

"Yeah, scared the heck out of me too," Stanley agreed. "And maybe it learnt Clarissa a lesson."

"Well, just before she left she asked me to tell Mary she loved her," Rosie said, "so I think maybe things are on the mend."

"That's fine then," he said. "That's just fine."

The glass sliding doors opened again and Katie Brennan walked through them. She looked quickly around the room, saw Rosie and Stanley and hurried to them. "How's Mary doing?" she asked, sitting next to them.

Stanley told her what he'd told Rosie and she sighed with relief.

"So, how did it happen?" she asked.

"There were some papers on the floor in the kitchen," Rosie said. "Mary didn't see them and she stepped on one and slipped backward. She caught her head on the corner of the butcher-block counter."

"Ouch," Katie said, wincing. "I bet that hurt."

"She cut her head, so there was blood everywhere," Stanley added. "Knocked her out for a while too."

"She lost consciousness?" Katie asked. "Well, that makes it a little more serious. I'm glad they're doing the CT scan."

They sat in silence for a few moments, the television running a cable news channel in the background. Finally, Katie turned to Rosie and Stanley and asked, "So, who's watching Clarissa?"

Rosie started. "Why, you are, aren't you?"

"What?" Katie exclaimed.

"Clarissa came downstairs after Mary went to the hospital and told me you called and asked her to come over to your house, so I could come to the hospital," Rosie said, her voice filled with concern.

Katie shook her head. "I never called," she said. "I just found out about Mary because Maggie came into the house and told me she was in the hospital."

"Could Maggie have invited her?" Stanley suggested. "Could she be there and you just didn't know?"

Katie pulled out her cell phone and called her house. "Andy, it's Mom," she said. "Please ask Maggie to come to the phone."

They all waited, their hearts in their throats, until Maggie answered. "Hi Mom," she said.

"Maggie, is Clarissa there with you?" she asked.

"No, Mom," Maggie said. "She's not here."

"Thank you," Katie said, shaking her head at Rosie and Stanley. "I want you to get your brothers and start looking around the neighborhood for her. I'll be home soon."

Stanley stood up and walked to the doors that separated the waiting room from the exam rooms. The nurse at the entrance looked up from her computer screen. "Can I help you?"

"I gotta talk to Police Chief Alden right away," he said. "There's another emergency at his home."

She nodded. "Just push the button on the wall for access," she said. "He's waiting in exam room three."

Stanley did as she said and the doors opened automatically. He rushed down the wide corridor and quickly found the room. Pausing outside the door, he knocked sharply.

"Come in," Bradley called.

Stanley pushed open the door and saw Bradley sitting alone in the room. "Where's Mary?" Stanley asked.

"Getting her CT scan," Bradley replied.

"We got another problem," Stanley said. "Clarissa's run away."

Standing and dropping the magazine he'd been leafing through, Bradley stared at Stanley as though he couldn't believe what he'd just said. "Run away?"

"Yeah, she told Rosie the Brennans had invited her over," he explained. "But Katie Brennan just arrived to check on Mary, and she never called Clarissa. She called her house, just to see if Clarissa was playing with Maggie. But Maggie told her Clarissa wasn't there. She's got her boys searching the neighborhood."

"Mike," Bradley said, looking over at the guardian angel who had jumped up as soon as Stanley came in. "Can you check on her?"

Mike shook his head, sadly. "She's made a decision she knows is wrong," he said. "At this point, I can't see or do anything unless she prays for help."

"Well, damn," Bradley muttered. "Mike, you stay with Mary. I've got to go find Clarissa. Make Mary stay put. We'll find her."

Mike nodded. "I'll keep her here," he said.

Grabbing his coat, he nodded. "Thanks Mike. Stanley, let's go."

Chapter Fifty-two

Ray dropped the newspaper in his lap and looked over at the GPS tracking screen, the alert alarm was going off. The Alden kid was moving. He pulled out of the parking lot at Read Park and headed down American Street toward his target. *She's moving pretty quickly*, he thought, *she's not walking.*

He drove slowly, staying a couple blocks away from the moving target. *Don't be too eager,* he cautioned himself, *you don't want to have to deal with her dad.*

He watched the indicator move across the screen into a neighborhood behind the Lincoln Mall. *What the hell is she doing back there?*

The streets behind the Lincoln Mall were circular, one leading into the other. They were not often traveled, and it was fairly difficult to remain anonymous once you pulled onto the street. Ray knew that he would have to wait until she reached her destination before he could follow.

Pulling into the far end of the Lincoln Mall, in front of the now empty supermarket, he found a parking spot that was hidden from the street and placed his car in park. He pulled out the plastic bag he'd placed under the passenger seat and put it on top of the seat. The washcloth soaked in chloroform was still damp.

Closing his eyes for a moment, he fantasized about her capture. He would simply walk up behind her and place the washcloth over her nose and mouth. She would struggle. His smile widened – he loved when they struggled. He would pull her closer to him, so he could feel her struggles against his body. Then, when it was almost too much to bear, when he was almost ready for release, she would lay limp in his arms.

Taking a deep breath, he allowed the erotic tension to seep from his body. He couldn't think of the pleasure yet; he had to have a clear head to catch her. She would be his last for a while. He would spend the entire night enjoying her, and in the morning, he would tend to his garden one last time before leaving town.

He watched the indicator slow and then finally stop in front of an address on Winter Drive. He waited a few moments, then put his car into drive and smiled to himself. She was nearly his.

Chapter Fifty-three

Clarissa slowed down as she got closer to her old house. The surrounding houses had changed since her mom and she had run away two years ago. She slid to a stop and straddled the bike, just looking at her home from a house away. Someone had painted it. Her mom's flower pots weren't on the front porch. The curtains over the big window in the front room were different. Would her dad still be in a house that wasn't theirs anymore?

She slid one leg over the center bar and walked the bike closer to the house. "Dad?" she whispered, not quite sure how she should be doing this. "Dad, can you hear me?"

She wheeled the bike closer, up the front path and to the porch. "Dad, it's Clarissa, I need you," she whispered urgently. "Please show me that you're here."

She looked around, studying any little detail that might prove her dad was nearby. The leaves on the lilac bush rustled and she moved closer, but then a small bird flew out of the branches. The gutters on the porch clattered, but when she looked up, she saw a squirrel running along the roof with a nut in its mouth. "Dad, you have to be here," she repeated. "I need to talk to you. I need to see you."

218

She waited, looking all around, but nothing happened.

Then the front door opened behind her. She twirled around with expectation and a little fear filling her heart. "Da..." she froze.

Her dad wasn't at the door; instead a young girl about her age stood on the porch. "Hi," the girl said. "Are you lost?"

Clarissa shook her head. "No, I'm not," she replied. "I used to live here and I was...looking for something."

"Oh," the girl replied brightly. "We've lived here for a month now. It's a very nice house. But we didn't find anything. What are you looking for?"

"Um, it's not important," Clarissa said. "I just was passing by and I thought I'd check."

"Where's your mom?"

"She's in the..." Clarissa stopped. She was going to tell her where Mary was; why hadn't she thought about her mother first? "She's dead. She died a few months ago."

"Oh, I'm so sorry," the girl exclaimed. "That would be awful. Where's your dad?"

An image of Bradley flashed into her mind, but she shook her head to clear it. "My dad died two years ago," she said firmly, trying to block Mary and Bradley from her thoughts.

"So you're an orphan, just like Annie," the girl said.

"No...I mean, yes. I mean...it's complicated."

"Are you all by yourself?"

Tears pricked at the back of Clarissa's eyes. *Yes*, she thought, *I am all by myself.*

She nodded. "Sort of."

"Lydia, why are standing there with the door open?" a woman's voice called from inside the house.

The little girl turned her head and shouted, "Mom, there's an orphan girl outside who used to live here."

"No, please," Clarissa said.

But it was too late; the mother was already standing behind her daughter on the porch. "Who are you?" she asked.

"I'm Clarissa," she replied, deciding not to add her last name.

"Well, Clarissa, do you want to come inside?" she asked. "It's getting dark. I could call someone for you."

Clarissa shook her head. "No, that's okay," she replied. "I should get going anyway."

"Where are you going?" the woman insisted.

"Um, probably back home," she lied.

"Young lady, I can tell when someone is not telling me the truth," she said. "I insist you come in, so we can call your folks."

Slipping her leg back over the center bar, she backed the bike up. "Really, I'll be fine," she said.

"I can drive you somewhere," the woman insisted, stepping forward on the porch.

"No thank you," Clarissa called as she pushed the bike back to the sidewalk and turned it away from the house. She jumped on the bike and pedaled quickly down the street.

The woman stood on the porch and watched her, shaking her head. *That little girl is frightened of something,* she thought, *I wonder if there's an Amber Alert out for her?*

She started to turn into the house when a movement caught her eye. She turned and watched a car moving slowly down the street, the driver's eyes on the departing little girl. She pulled out her cell phone and took a photo of the license plate. She'd save that just in case there was an Amber Alert about the child.

Chapter Fifty-four

Mary was wheeled down the corridor from the radiology section toward the examination room by the technician who performed the CT scan. "I'll finish processing the test and get the results to the radiologist as quickly as possible," she said. "Then he'll call it down to the emergency room doctor."

"Thank you. In the meantime, can I change back into my own clothes?" she asked, fingering the hospital gown she was wearing. "Not that I don't love the style."

The technician laughed and nodded. "Yes, I think we're done poking at you for the time being," she said. "Go ahead and change."

Mary climbed out of the wheelchair and nodded. "Thanks again," she said.

The technician closed the door behind her and Mary turned to Mike, standing next to her bed. "Where's Bradley?" she asked.

"Well, there was a little misunderstanding at home," Mike replied. "It seems that we've misplaced Clarissa."

"What?" Mary exclaimed.

Mike hurried over. "Okay, you sit down and calm down, okay?" he said. "Bradley, Rosie, Stanley and the entire Brennan crew are searching for her. They'll find her in no time."

"How could this happen?"

"Well, Clarissa told Rosie that the Brennans had called and wanted her to stay with them, so Rosie could be here with you," Mike explained. "But when Katie showed up here and had no knowledge of the conversation, they put two and two together."

"What did Maggie say?" Mary asked.

"Katie called Maggie and asked her if Clarissa was there," Mike said. "Maggie said no."

"Do you honestly believe that Maggie doesn't know more about this or doesn't at least have a clue where Clarissa might be going?" she insisted.

Mike slapped his forehead. "Of course she does," he said. "Those two are as thick as thieves."

"Okay, I'll get dressed and then let's get going," Mary said, pulling her clothes out of the closet.

"No," Mike said. "I promised Bradley that you would stay put until the doctor released you. So, you need to stay put."

"But they need me," she insisted.

"I'll go talk to Maggie," he said. "I can pull angel rank on her and get her to confess. Then I'll tell Bradley anything I learn. In the meantime, you sit here and wait. Okay?"

She sighed loudly. "Fine," she said. "But if you don't find her within thirty minutes, I'm stealing an ambulance and going out searching on my own."

Mike chuckled, "Yes, momma bear, I understand."

As soon as Mike faded away, Mary quickly dressed, hesitating a couple of times when she felt a little dizzy. She finally finished and looked around the room for her purse and her cell phone. She needed to call Bradley to find out what was going on. She searched the closet and all of the drawers, and then realized the awful truth. "Well, crap," she said. "They didn't bring my purse."

She sat down on the bed and fumed. "They better bring me some news, fast."

Chapter Fifty-five

Clarissa hurried down the street before the woman on the porch could call the police. She didn't want to go to jail. She rode to the end of the block and stopped, looking up and down the intersecting streets. But where was she going to go? She couldn't contact her dad; she didn't have any other friends in town. She sighed; the only place she could go was home.

She started to turn the bike when she saw the car glide to the curb. "Hello there Clarissa," Ray Giles said, hanging out of the window. "Your father sent me over to get you. He said it was getting dark and he needed you to come home now."

Clarissa shook her head. "No, that's okay," she said, her heart tripping in her chest. "I'll just ride home by myself."

"But there's been an accident," he said. "Your mother has been hurt. They need you to hurry home."

How did he know that Mary had been hurt? she wondered. *Could he be telling the truth?*

He watched her hesitate and opened the car door, the washcloth hidden in his hand. "She's hurt badly," he continued, stepping onto the curb. "She was in a car accident."

That was all she needed to hear. Clarissa jumped down on the pedal and wheeled away from him as fast as she could. "Get back here," he shouted. "You get back here right now."

Clarissa sped down the sidewalk, knowing she couldn't beat him back home. She crossed the road at the small cul-de-sac on Winter Drive and rode alongside one of the houses. She crossed through the backyard and into the adjacent backyard and then up onto Bailey Avenue. She rode across the street and then peered down driveways to find a house that didn't have a fence. Finally, halfway down the block she found a house whose yard backed up to another yard without a fence, she turned her bike alongside the house and drove through both yards to end up on Wise Street.

At the end of the driveway, she paused to catch her breath and decide what she was going to do next. She couldn't make it home; it was too far away and no one was there. Suddenly she heard the sound of a helicopter and saw that it was very low to the ground. Of course, the hospital was just at the end of this street and a little way down Stephenson. She could make it to the hospital. Mary and Bradley would be there. They would save her.

She jumped back on her bike and pedaled in the direction of the hospital, pausing only to wait for the light on Stephenson. She turned into the parking lot and rode along the back to the emergency room, dropping her bike outside the door and running into the lobby.

To her dismay the waiting room was empty. Where were Stanley and Rosie? They were supposed to be here.

She saw car lights reflected against the glass doors and turned around. Her blood ran cold as she saw Ray's car slowly drive past the emergency room, his eyes meeting hers. As she watched him pull to a stop, she knew she had to find Mary.

A nurse, pushing a gurney, came out through the large brown doors that led to the examination rooms. Keeping herself hidden, Clarissa waited until the gurney passed and slipped through the doors as they were closing. She hurried down the corridor, praying she could find Mary before anyone found her and threw her out.

"Mary," she called, as she walked near the rooms. "Mary."

"Clarissa?"

Clarissa's heart leapt with joy when she heard Mary's voice. When the door opened and Mary stepped into the hallway, Clarissa ran to her and wrapped her arms around her waist. "I'm so sorry," she cried. "I'm so sorry."

Mary guided the little girl into the room, closing the door behind her, and then knelt down and wrapped her arms around her daughter. "I'm so glad you're safe," she said. "Everyone is out looking for you. You should never run away."

Suddenly the alarms in the emergency area sounded. Ear-spitting sirens sounded throughout the floor.

Clarissa raised her head, her face wet with tears. "The bad man was after me," she shouted. "So I came here. The bad man wanted to snatch me."

"What bad man?" Mary asked.

"This one," Ray said, stepping into the room with a gun pointed at Mary.

Chapter Fifty-six

Mary stood up and pushed Clarissa behind her, shielding her. "There is no way you are taking my child," Mary yelled above the noise.

Ray smiled and shook his head. "No, I have a much better idea," he said. "I'll take both of you."

Mary moved into a defensive stance. "You'll have to get through me first," she said, praying that she would be strong enough to fight him.

He stepped forward and threw a punch, Mary deflected it, but he was too fast and slapped her on the side of her head with his gun. Dropping to her knees, Mary fought to remain conscious. "No," she screamed, fighting to stand. "Stay away from her."

"Too late," Ray said, stepping back, Clarissa tucked against him, the gun at her neck. "Now you're going to do exactly what I say or this little girl dies."

Mary nodded, wiping the blood from the cut on her face onto the bed sheet. "Okay, whatever you say, just don't hurt Clarissa."

"You're going to walk with us down the corridor," he said. "With the fire alarm I started, they're going to expect everyone to evacuate the building, so no one will stop us. You don't talk to anyone; you just walk to my car parked right outside the door. Got it?"

Mary nodded and Ray motioned with his head for her to lead the way.

He was right; the hospital staff was so busy helping non-ambulatory patients out of their rooms they didn't even notice the three of them leaving. He pulled out of the parking lot just as the fire trucks came pulling in. "That will keep everyone busy for a little while," he said, looking over at Mary and Clarissa huddled next to him in the front seat.

"Now, the next thing you're going to do," he said, motioning with the gun he still held in his left hand, "is to make yourself a little more agreeable."

He motioned to the washcloth on the floor of the car in front of Mary. "Pick it up and put it on Clarissa's face," he said. "Hold it there until she passes out."

"You don't need Clarissa," Mary said. "I'll do whatever you want me to do. We can drop Clarissa off at the house. You don't need her."

"I need her alright," he growled. "Especially now, there ain't no way either of you are going to escape. Now, either you do it, or I do it."

Mary picked up the washcloth and held it next to Clarissa's face.

Burying her face into Mary's arm, she turned her face slightly, so she didn't inhale the full effect of the sweet-smelling liquid. She closed her eyes and went limp, pretending she was asleep. Mary pulled the cloth from her face. "She's out," she said.

"Good, now put it on your face," he said.

"Do you think I'd leave my daughter even if I had a chance to run?" she asked. "If you have Clarissa, you have me."

"Lady, I think you'd crawl up inside me and turn me inside out to save your daughter," he said. "And I'm not going to give you the chance. Besides, I like my women dizzy and helpless. It makes getting to know them much more interesting."

Nausea swept through Mary at his words and she had to swallow to hold it back.

"Washcloth, now," he commanded.

Mary brought the washcloth to her face and breathed it in; she tried not to respond, but the effects of her concussion and the chloroform were too much. In a matter of minutes, she was passed out next to Clarissa.

"Now, we're going to have some real fun," Ray said, turning down the road toward his house.

Chapter Fifty-seven

Maggie was huddled in the window seat of the big window in her room, staring out into the darkening evening sky. Mike appeared in her room behind her and watched her for a few moments without speaking.

"It's scary out there," Mike finally said, his voice soft.

She nodded, not startled by him at all.

"How long have you known I was here?" he asked, moving up alongside her.

"I knew you'd come," she said. "'Cause I was praying real hard."

"It's always a good thing to pray, Maggie," he said. "But it's also good to tell the truth. All the truth."

"But I promised," she said, looking up at him, worry evident on her face.

"And sometimes we make promises that we realize are not good ones to keep," he said. "Promises that can hurt someone are not good promises. Promises that cover up lies are not good promises."

She nodded. "So I can break those kinds, right?"

"You need to break those kinds to save your friends."

"Clarissa wanted to find her dad," she explained. "She wanted to talk to him, so she went to her old house."

"Was she walking?"

Maggie shook her head. "I gave her my bike," she said. "So she could get there faster."

"Thank you, Maggie," Mike said. "You did the right thing."

"Find her, Mike," Maggie said. "Please hurry and find her."

Chapter Fifty-eight

Bradley was driving his cruiser slowly up and down the streets near their house, searching for his little girl. His stomach was tied up in knots. He thought she was fine. He thought she was just going through normal childhood adjustments. He never dreamed she was so unhappy she would run away. "Clarissa," he called from the window.

Mike appeared in the seat next to him. "Maggie told me that Clarissa was going to her old house," he said. "She wanted to see if she could find her dad."

Without a word, Bradley turned on the sirens and sped toward Winter Drive. They parked at the curb and Bradley ran up the path to the house. He rapped sharply on the door. A woman quickly answered, looked at his uniform and asked, "Are you here about that little girl? The one on the pink bike with the white basket?"

He nodded. "Yes, I am," he said. "Is she still here?"

"No, like I told them when I called it in," she said. "It just seemed strange that a girl that young would be out all by herself, and then when that car started following her. Well, it just made my blood run cold."

"Car?" Bradley asked. "What car?"

"The car that was waiting down the street and took off as soon as she starting riding away," she said. "I waited on the porch and watched them for a while. The man tried to coax her into his car, but she hightailed it out of there on her bike."

"Do you have a description of the car or the man?" he asked.

"I have a photo," she said. "Took it with my phone. Here take a look."

Picking up his radio, he called the license plate number into the dispatcher, trying to keep his voice calm as sheer terror overwhelmed him. He looked at the photo again and was sure the man driving was Ray Giles.

Handing the woman back her phone, he thanked her. "You have probably saved this little girl's life," he said, his voice becoming hoarse with emotion. "Thank you so much."

"I hope you find her," she called after him.

He ran to the car and threw it into gear.

"You need to call Mary," Mike said, "or she'll go crazy."

He punched a button on his radio. "Hey, this is Alden, can you connect me to the Emergency Room?"

He waited a few moments for the connection to go through. "ER," the woman's voice said.

"Hey, Audrey, this is Chief Alden," he said. "I need to speak with Mary. She's in exam room three."

"Hold on just a moment, Chief," she said. "I'll connect you to the Nurse's Station back there."

He sped down the road as the connection was made. "Hello, Chief Alden, I'm afraid your wife is no longer in her room," the nurse said. "But it's been crazy here. Someone pulled a fire alarm and we had to evacuate the building. We think it was a child, because we found a pink bike abandoned just outside the emergency room doors."

"Clarissa had Maggie's pink bike," Mike said.

"Did anyone see her leave?" Bradley asked.

"Well, now that you mention it," she replied. "One of the nurses thought she saw Mary leave with a little girl and a man. But I told her that couldn't be Mary."

"Thank you," Bradley said, disconnecting the call and feeling sick to his stomach. "I think Giles might have both of them."

"The kidnapper?" Mike exclaimed.

"The woman at the house took a picture of a car following Clarissa," Bradley said, his jaw tight. "It was Ray Giles. I know it."

"So, are we heading to Giles's house?" Mike asked.

"And if he's hurt either of them..." Bradley didn't finish his sentence, but Mike understood.

Chapter Fifty-nine

Clarissa concentrated on breathing evenly and playing like she was asleep when Ray lifted her from his car and carried her through the garage. She could feel light on her face when he walked into his house and could tell they were going downstairs. Then he just dumped her on a hard bed, with her backpack digging into her back, and strapped her down, so she couldn't move. Waiting until she heard him walk away, she opened her eyes and looked around the room.

It looked like a classroom. There were chalkboards against one wall and large maps of the world against another. A cursive alphabet border ran along the wall, right under the ceiling, and a bookcase filled with children's books was in the corner. There were some old wooden student's desks in a single row along one side of the room and a teacher's desk sat at the very front with a long yardstick and some rope sitting on top.

The basement windows were covered with dark paper and the only way to get into the room was the door that led back upstairs.

She heard footsteps and closed her eyes, keeping her breath deep and even. The door banged open and she nearly jumped, but she clutched her hands into fists, stayed quiet and listened.

"Well, now, you're going to be a lot more fun than my usual students," he whispered to Mary. "It's just too bad that we only have tonight to have you learn your lessons. By tomorrow you will be another bit of compost for my garden, buried under a pine tree."

Clarissa squeezed her fists tighter to keep from crying.

"Now, let me tie you up nice and tight and then we'll let the effects of the chloroform wear off a little. That way you can enjoy the fun as much as I will. Then after I finish with you, I'll let you watch me teach your daughter a thing or two. I think you'll get a kick out of that," he laughed softly. "I know I will."

Clarissa didn't really understand what he meant, but she knew he was going to hurt Mary first. She concentrated on breathing softly, even when Ray came back to the bed she was on. He placed his hand on her cheek and stroked it, then slowly moved it down her arm and over to her waist. She shivered involuntarily and her breath caught in her throat.

He lifted his hand and was silent. Did he realize she wasn't really asleep?

She tried to imagine she was in her bedroom, tucked inside her own bed. She imagined that Bradley was sleeping in the rocking chair next to her bed, a book in his lap. She felt her body relax and she was able to resume the slow rhythmic pace, breathing in and out.

"Your body must already enjoy my caresses," Ray said. "Good. You're going to be a fast learner."

He swept his hand over her body one last time and then walked away, closing the door behind him. She waited until she heard him climb all of the stairs before she opened her eyes. Lifting her head, she could see Mary strapped onto the bed across the room. "Mary," she whispered. "Mary, can you hear me?"

But there was no response. Mary was still unconscious, the white bandage on her head and the new bruising on her face reminding Clarissa just what Mary had been through that day.

She thought about Mike, but she figured she had messed up so much that even God was angry with her. A tear slipped down her cheek. How could she have been so dumb?

She closed her eyes for a moment, blinking back tears.

"You aren't dumb and God isn't mad at you," Mike said.

Her eyes springing open, she smiled in relief. "Mike," she whispered. "Help us."

He shook his head. "I'm really sorry, sweetheart, but I can't," he said. "God isn't mad, but He does follow the rules. You made choices you know were wrong, and now you have to face the consequences. And you have to figure your own way out."

"But it wasn't Mary's fault," she said. "She didn't do anything. She shouldn't get hurt."

"That's the problem when people make bad choices," he said. "Often innocent people get hurt too."

"But can't you do anything?" she pleaded.

"I can tell you that you have the ability to rescue yourself and Mary," he said as he faded away. "And I know you can do it."

She threw herself back on her backpack in frustration and got poked for her efforts. "Ouch," she said, sitting back up and rolling to the side.

She looked down and saw the shard from Mary's chest was poking out of the pocket. It was so sharp it had cut clean through the canvas backpack. Clarissa's eyes widened and she worked on getting her hand up and through the strap on the bed to grab hold of the shard. Holding it carefully, she drew it back and forth across the heavy cotton strap until it started to fray. She kept cutting, back and forth, until finally it snapped apart.

Quickly sliding off her bed, Clarissa ran to Mary's bed. "Mary," she whispered, and then she paused for a second. "I'm here. I'm going to get you out."

Mary had been strapped down with two belts of cotton, so Clarissa started to saw on the top one. Soon the top one started to fray and after a few more strokes, it too snapped apart. She moved down to the bottom of the bed, where the strap was over her legs. She dug deeply into the cotton, cutting her own hand with the effort, but she didn't stop. She didn't know how much time she had until Ray came back down.

Finally, the band broke. Clarissa stuffed the shard in her pocket and hurried to the top of the bed. "Mom. Mom," she called. "You have to wake up."

Mary moaned softly. "Clarissa?"

A moment of relief washed over Clarissa. "Please, Mom, you have to wake up before Ray comes back downstairs."

Mary opened her eyes and struggled to sit up. "Did you do this?" she asked. "Did you get us loose?"

Nodding, Clarissa smiled up at Mary. "I just pretended I was asleep," she said. "So I could help you."

Mary wrapped her arms around her daughter and hugged her. "Now I have to figure out part two of the plan," she muttered to herself.

Clarissa looked around the room. "Well, he has to come through that door to get us," she said. "We could hide behind the door and then hit him with something."

Mary looked around the room too, searching for a weapon. Finally she came upon an old wooden baseball bat sitting in the corner; she hurried over and picked it up. It was still in good shape, and it was solid oak. "I think this would work," she said.

They heard him stirring upstairs. Mary turned to her daughter and put her arm on her shoulder. "Clarissa, I need you to get back on your table, so when he opens the door, he thinks everything is still fine," she said, searching her daughter's eyes. "Can you do that? I know it's going to be scary."

241

"It's fine, Mom," she said. "I know you'll take him out."

Mary hugged her once again. "I love you," she whispered.

With her lower lip trembling, Clarissa looked up into Mary's face. "I love you too."

They heard footsteps on the staircase. Clarissa flew across the room and slid onto the bed, sliding the strap over her body. Mary braced herself behind the door, holding the bat over her shoulder.

The door opened wide and Ray stepped into the room, looked at Clarissa and smiled, then he turned toward Mary's bed.

Mary whipped the bat around with all of her might, but Ray saw it coming and shifted his body. The bat glanced off his back, throwing him forward, but he was still standing. "You little bitch," he yelled, charging at Mary.

She swung the bat again, this time connecting with his arm, but he still moved forward, tackling her and crushing her against the wall. The bat dropped from her hand as she fought him, punching and kicking, trying to connect in any way she could. But he was stronger, deflecting many of her attempts and landing more of his own. Mary didn't know how long she would be able to keep this up.

"Run, Clarissa, run," she screamed, as she put all of her strength into an upper cut.

Clarissa slid off the table and saw Mary, crushed against the wall, being pummeled by the evil man. She slipped the shard out of her pocket, gripped it in her hand and ran forward, shoving the shard into his thigh.

Screaming, he whipped around. Clarissa jumped back and ran toward the table.

Mary bent down and found the bat at her feet.

"I'm going to kill you," he yelled, stepping forward just as the baseball bat connected with the side of his head.

He turned back to Mary, dazed, but even angrier. "But I'm going to kill you first," he screamed.

The click of a gun's trigger echoed in the room. "I don't think you're going to be killing anyone anymore," Bradley said, his gun aimed at Ray's head. "But if you'd like to give me a reason to shoot, please, be my guest."

Ray backed away from Mary and raised his hands over his head. "You can get me for kidnapping and assault," he said. "But you've got nothing else on me."

"The murder of Nick Sears," Bradley said.

"You got any evidence?" he asked with a smirk.

Clarissa ran around the room and stood next to Mary, wrapping her arms around her. "He buried the girls in his yard, Daddy," she said. "He buried them under his trees. He said he was going to bury Mom and me there too."

Ray's angry glance at Clarissa confirmed the accuracy of her story.

"Well, I guess we do have something else on you. Good job, Clarissa," he said, sending a quick look of approval to his daughter. "Now I want you on the floor, Giles, spread-eagle."

Chapter Sixty

"I really think I could get up," Mary complained from her bed.

"The doctor said if we wanted to keep you here instead of in the hospital, you have to have complete bed rest," Bradley said.

"But we don't even know if I have a concussion yet," she said. "They haven't even called."

Bradley leaned over and gently ran a finger over his wife's bruised face. "Darling, I don't need a hospital report to tell me that…"

"Bradley," Mary warned him, as she watched Clarissa slip into their bedroom.

"That really bad man," Bradley inserted, "used you like a punching bag."

"She punched him too," Clarissa added, defending her mother. "She punched him hard and hit him with a bat. Right on the side of his head."

Mary smiled down at Clarissa. "But only after Clarissa stabbed him in the leg to draw him off of me," she said. "She probably saved my life."

Clarissa shook her head. "But you wouldn't have even been there if not for me."

"Come up here on the bed next to me," Mary said, holding her arms out to Clarissa.

She climbed up onto the bed and lay in Mary's arms. Mary hugged her and kissed her on the top of her head. "I don't want you ever to think what happened to me was your fault," she said. "It was Ray Giles's fault. He was the bad man."

Then she loosened her hold on Clarissa and looked down at her face. "But there are some things we are going to have to do, if we want to be a family," she said.

"What?" Clarissa asked, looking up at Mary.

"Well, we need to make sure we talk to each other," she said. "Especially when we are afraid or confused. If we don't talk, we can't help each other. We can't learn to trust each other."

Clarissa nodded.

"I want you to put the photo of your parents on your nightstand," Mary said, "if you want to. They loved you and they were wonderful parents. And your dad and I are both so grateful they took such good care of you. We don't want you ever to feel you have to forget about them."

"Are they part of our family?" Clarissa asked.

"Of course they are, because that's what families do," she replied. "They love each other. And they protect each other."

"Like you did at the hospital," Clarissa said.

"And like you did when you cut the straps and stabbed Ray," Mary said.

"There's an old Chinese proverb that says when you save someone's life, you are responsible for that person for the rest of their life," Bradley said.

"So it looks like you two are responsible for each other."

"But you saved us when you came in with your gun," Clarissa said. "So you're responsible for both of us."

"Yes, for both of us," Mary said with a twinkle in her eye. "Now won't that be fun?"

"So, we are all responsible for each other," Bradley said. "That's a pretty good start for a family, don't you think?"

"Yes," Clarissa agreed. "I like that."

Mary hugged her again. "Good, I like that too."

"Clarissa, Bradley," Rosie called from downstairs. "I have a plate of get-well cookies and glasses of milk that need to be brought upstairs."

"Cool," Clarissa said, sliding from the bed. "I love get-well cookies."

Mary laughed, "So do I."

Clarissa ran from the room and they could both hear her running down the stairs to the kitchen. Bradley moved up closer to the top of the bed and sat next to Mary. He stroked her forehead gently and then picked up her hand and brought it to his lips. "How are you feeling, really?" he asked.

"I'm sore from head to toe," she said with a soft smile. "But my heart feels full and wonderful."

He lifted her hand and kissed it again. Then he just held it for a few moments. "I can't begin to describe the terror I felt when I discovered Ray had both of you," he said. "I thought my life was going to end."

She stroked his face gently and nodded. "I knew you would come and rescue us."

"I love you, Mary O'Reilly Alden," he said, leaning forward and kissing her tenderly on the lips.

"I love you, Bradley Alden," she replied.

Suddenly a thought came to her mind and she sat up in bed. "Celia," she exclaimed. "Did anyone call Celia?"

Bradley nodded and placed his hands on her shoulders, gently easing her back against the pillows. "Yes, darling, I called Celia when the good doctor was making sure you were okay," he said. "She was surprised, of course, that it was Ray, and she was angry."

"Angry is good," Mary said. "I should call her..."

"I told her you would call her tomorrow," he interrupted. "And that we would be sending a forensics team out to his place tomorrow to start careful excavation of the grounds."

Nodding, she finally relaxed. "Thank you," she said, sliding her arms around his shoulders, "for letting her know."

He bent closer and pressed a kiss against her lips. "Now, where were we?"

"Daddy," Clarissa called from downstairs, "I need you to help carry the milk."

Bradley shook his head, smiled and stood up. "It's never going to be boring, is it?" he asked.

248

She shook her head. "No, I don't think so."

Her cell phone rang as Bradley left the room. "Hello?"

"May I speak with Mary Alden please?"

"This is Mary Alden," Mary replied.

"Hello, Mary, this is Freeport Hospital with your lab results," the woman on the other end said. "There is no internal bleeding, but you did have a minor concussion. You can take acetaminophen, but nothing stronger, and no ibuprofen because of your condition."

"My condition?" Mary asked, worried.

"Oh, you did know that you are pregnant, didn't you?"

About the author:

Terri Reid lives near Freeport, the home of the Mary O'Reilly Mystery Series, and loves a good ghost story. She lives in a hundred-year-old farmhouse complete with its own ghost. She loves hearing from her readers at author@terrireid.com.

Books by Terri Reid:

Loose Ends – A Mary O'Reilly Paranormal Mystery (Book One)

Good Tidings – A Mary O'Reilly Paranormal Mystery (Book Two)

Never Forgotten – A Mary O'Reilly Paranormal Mystery (Book Three)

Final Call – A Mary O'Reilly Paranormal Mystery (Book Four)

Darkness Exposed – A Mary O'Reilly Paranormal Mystery (Book Five)

Natural Reaction – A Mary O'Reilly Paranormal Mystery (Book Six)

Secret Hollows – A Mary O'Reilly Paranormal Mystery (Book Seven)

Broken Promises – A Mary O'Reilly Paranormal Mystery (Book Eight)

Twisted Paths – A Mary O'Reilly Paranormal Mystery (Book Nine)

Veiled Passages – A Mary O'Reilly Paranormal Mystery (Book Ten)

Bumpy Roads – A Mary O'Reilly Paranormal Mystery (Book Eleven)

The Ghosts Of New Orleans – A Paranormal
Research and Containment Division (PRCD) Case
File

CPSIA information can be obtained
at www.ICGtesting.com
Printed in the USA
LVHW08s0507230918
591047LV00038B/512/P